BOOTY CALL

AINSLEY BOOTH

WWW.AINSLEYBOOTH.COM

I know what I'm doing when I text Scott at four in the morning.
He knows what I'm doing, too.
That's why he shows up twenty-three minutes later, freshly showered with a condom in his pocket and a barely dissolved breath mint on his tongue.
I smirk as he looms over me. "You are such a dirty old man."
"We need to stop doing this."
"Why?"
"Because you're twenty and I'm not. Because I want to take you on a fucking date and you won't. Because we wind up yelling at each other half the time."
"But the rest of the time you're inside me and it feels so good, right?"
His eyes darken and I don't need to look down to know he's hard for me.
I love that.
This isn't me. That's the crazy part.
I'm taunting my sister's ex-bodyguard, working him into a lather in the hopes that he'll fuck me so hard I won't be able to walk straight tomorrow.

It's a dangerous game—my new favorite, because it's secret. This pleasure? I hold it close.
I haven't told my sister, and she's my best friend.
I never will, either. Because when I do, this will end.
And I'm definitely not ready for this to end.
We've only just gotten started.

This is the complete story of Ali Dashford Reid and Scott Mayfair. The Forbidden Bodyguard series continues…

Also in this series:
Hate F*@k (Cole and Hailey)
Dirty Love (Wilson and Tabitha)
Wicked Sin (Taylor and Luke)
Filthy Liar (Jason and Melinda)

Booty Call

Ali and Scott

part one

New York

[1]

ALISON

Happy birthday to me.

I'm supposed to be having an epic shop-a-thon with my sister in SoHo, but now we're stuck at the Apple store because Hailey needs someone to fix her phone. Her fiancé Cole will have a fit if she's off the grid.

God forbid. It's not like she isn't being shadowed everywhere by her bodyguard—big, brooding Scott Mayfair, of the dark, dirty looks and annoyingly consistent hands-off-Alison attitude—for our "girls weekend". But her phone stopped working at lunch, so now Hailey's waiting for a so-called genius to help her fix it.

Me?

I'm going to take advantage of the fact that Scott can't leave Hailey's side and go buy myself a present.

"I'm just heading around the corner," I murmur to my sister. She knows where I'm going. Every time we come to the city, I visit the Agent Provocateur store on Mercer Street. It's become my little ritual.

Alison Dashford Reid, all grown up and secretly wearing something naughty beneath her studious university student uniform of yoga pants and hoodies. Although that's not what I'm wearing today. While it works for Washington...New York City, not so much. Not at the level that Hailey and I are playing this weekend.

I've got my Jimmy Choo fuck-me boots zipped over my skinny Sevens, and a wool jacket over a silk camisole, because it's February and there's only so much cold my nipples can take in the name of fashion.

I sling the skinny strap of my purse across my body and join the flow of Saturday afternoon shoppers. New York is unlike any other city in the world, and SoHo might be my favorite neighborhood in my favorite city. Narrow shops and cobblestone streets. It brings out the girly-girl in me, and I indulge that lucky bitch with pretty underwear.

Inside, Agent Provocateur is glossy black lacquer and sparkling crystal chandeliers. A sea of silk and lace. Black ribbons and satin cups. It oozes feminine power and celebrates all things sexy.

My private collection of lingerie is one step in the direction of claiming more of that attitude for myself.

One day soon, I'm going to be this woman.

I sigh. Maybe not *soon*. I have to keep my head down until I'm done with school and can leave Washington. Leave the toxic world of my parents behind and just be myself.

Be Alison, girl with silk panties. Girl with an easy, breezy attitude toward sex and men and life.

"Can I help you?" A smiling salesgirl approaches, and I'm glad I dressed up. I look the part of the rich socialite, and all afternoon I've been getting that treatment. Not normally something I care about one way or the other—and if pushed, I lean toward other. Because seriously, being rich just gives people the excuse to be depraved fucks.

And then have children, and ruin their lives with the depravity.

I shudder inside.

But on the outside, I just smile at the salesgirl. "I'm going to look around a bit. First time in a while since I've been in the store."

First time since all the weird shit went down with my sisters last year. Now I can't just get on the train and come to New York for the weekend. Now when I suggest a girls' trip, it's a full-on *thing*, complete with Scott tagging along if Cole is busy.

We made that mistake once in the fall. Ugh. Totally un-fun, although it did beat a totally awkward family Thanksgiving.

This trip wasn't my idea, even though it's my birthday weekend. But Hailey's got a gleam in her eye about a wedding dress, which means Cole's finally won their non-stop battle over whether or not to get married.

Well, not that there's a battle over getting *married*. Just a battle over the actual "getting hitched" moment. As in, Hailey doesn't want a wedding. Not one our mother can ruin.

So I bet they'll elope, which is totally fine.

After all the shit she's been through, Hailey deserves to be happy.

And if she wants to buy a non-wedding dress for a secret wedding that she's not telling me about just yet, I'll suck up a totally un-fun trip to the big city.

After all, when I get bored, I can always ditch the bodyguard and sneak into a lingerie shop.

I smirk to myself—which is when karma decides to punish me.

"Something funny, Miss Reid?" He must have caught the side of my face.

Damn it. I sigh and roll my eyes to the sparkly chandelier, keeping my back to Scott. My sister's bodyguard. My secret crush. My totally off-limits, no-fun babysitter for the weekend, apparently, since he's followed me, and not for any fun, dirty reasons. "How did you find me? Do I have a tracking device implanted under my skin?"

Scott laughs quietly and circles around the display until I've got a face full of cotton dress shirt and black suit jacket. Both fitted and stretched across strong shoulders.

A wide chest.

Probably a hard set of abs, but I've never gotten close enough to test that theory.

I don't look up at his face. Instead, I pretend to look at the panties on the far side of the table, right in front of his hips.

His package is pretty substantial, too. Definitely stretching the fabric there.

I blush, but I don't duck my head further.

I'm totally fine with Scott knowing that I'm thinking about his cock.

He's not fine with it, but that's his problem.

He clears his throat and crosses his arms, swinging a collection of our shopping bags in front of his body to hide what I hope is a monster reaction to me. "Your sister suggested I might find you in here."

"And you left Hailey alone to come find me?"

"Cole showed up. Turns out he had business in the city after all."

Of course he did. Which meant that our girls' weekend just turned into me being a third-wheel on a romantic getaway.

Fuck.

"Then I might head back to D.C." I say quietly. I'm not trying to hide the fact I'm disappointed. It's my birthday. I can be fucking disappointed if I want.

I can swear like a fucking sailor and pretend I'm not a Dean's List, finishing-school Good Girl, because it's my twentieth birthday and I can't even buy lingerie without my sister's drama intruding.

And since that *drama* won't let me check him out... yeah, I'm pouting.

"You can head home. If you want." His voice is...is...

I jerk my eyes up to his face.

He's mocking me.

Outrage surges through me, unexpectedly, at the barely contained laughter in his voice. I can feel my face turning red, twin dots of heat burning on my cheekbones. I pick up a complicated thong, with bonus straps that do nothing but torment the person looking at the wearer, probably, and I hold it up between us. "You don't think I should do that, *Scott*?" I put my own mocking spin on his name. "What should I do instead? You think I should stay here in the big city, and buy these panties, maybe wear them out tonight under a little black dress? Knowing full well there's not a chance in hell I'll get peeled out of them at the end of the night by a hot guy? Happy birthday, Alison. Here's to another year of bodyguard-enforced virginity."

I'm being a whiny brat. I don't care. It's been months of this rock star treatment, and seriously, it's overrated. We grew up in a wealthy family, so having private security isn't totally out my realm of understanding, but Hailey's relationship with one of Washington's top crisis management guys—and getting tangled up in a human trafficking ring—has taken shit to a whole new level.

It actually doesn't affect my everyday life. I go to school. I even have my own apartment now, having moved out of my parents' estate at Christmas time because there's only so much fucked-up drama one can handle and still stay on the Dean's List.

But it does affect every "sister thing" I want to do with Hailey.

Including celebrating my birthday.

So I stare at Scott, daring him—fucking *daring* him—to tell me that I can do anything I want, of course I can.

Because I can't.

He stares back, his face unreadable.

"I don't think Cole is planning on going out for dinner with you two, if that's your concern," he finally says gruffly, but I'm still pissed off. Anger sizzles under my skin and now I'm just thinking shit that's not fair and doesn't really matter. But that's the thing about feelings, right? Once you have them, you can't just un-have them.

Tears prick at the back of my eyelids, and *no*, that is not happening. I pinch the inside of my palm with my fingers and slowly roll my eyes back to the ceiling, exhaling as I tell myself to pull it together.

Let him think I'm a haughty bitch. I don't care.

"Miss Reid," he starts, and I drop my gaze, staring past him as I twirl the panties on the tip of my finger.

"I'm not a child. You can call me Alison, or Ms. Reid. Or nothing at all. That would be my preference." I swing past him and hold out the lace and ribbon scrap of nothing to the sales girl. "I'll take these with a matching 32C bra, please."

I shake my head when she asks if I'll need to try anything on.

While the thought of making Scott sit outside a change room would usually make me achy and wet, right now I'm not in the mood to play the tease. Not when it's not going to get me anywhere.

I'm not a child. I told him that. I told my parents the same thing when I moved into my own apartment.

One of these days, I'm going to start believing it for myself.

And until then, I'll fake it.

I've been doing that my entire life. I'm a pro.

After I pay for my purchases, I head for the door. Scott stands back, letting me move past him, but even though he hasn't said anything, I still feel unsettled. Like maybe I haven't had the last word.

He doesn't get to do that to me.

I am *not* a child. I won't be handled.

I stop and meet his gaze head-on. "Call the restaurant and change our reservation. Cole can join us. And you can, too."

"I'm fine at the bar...Ms. Reid." His jaw clenches, but that's the only reaction.

"I understand that." I lift my bag and wave it in the air. "But since my future brother-in-law won't let me wear this for anyone else, tonight I'm wearing these for you. Whether you like it or not."

[2]
SCOTT

AFTER THAT DANGEROUS-AS-HELL TAUNT, I give Alison a
wide berth as we leave the store. She's pissed at me and it's my
job not to react. If she needs an emotional punching bag, I guess
I can be that for her—to a point.

But right now, she's just giving me the ice-queen routine as
she sweeps into the chaos of New York City. Ideally, I'd want to
walk in front of her, watching for threats, but I'm not her bodyguard so I don't get to lay down that law of protection.

Unfortunately, walking behind her comes with its own set
of problems.

Like the fact that the jeans she's wearing should be illegal,
along with the panties she waved in my face. Snug as fuck, the
denim cups her ass as if taunting me. *See this, old man? You'd go
to jail for touching this. But we get to stroke her all day long.*

She's not actually jail-bait. Thank Christ for that.

But she's off-limits all the same—and not just because I work
for her sister's fiancé. Alison Dashford Reid is gorgeous, smart,
and fifteen years younger than me.

Well, fourteen now.

Happy Birthday, Miss Reid. Welcome to your twenties. My

dick thickens at the memory of how she pouted about her birthday dinner. I'd love to spank the brat right out of her. Another reason she's off-limits, because it wouldn't end with spanking. I'd punish her until her ass is rosy-red and she's panting all the good-girl apologies she learned at boarding school, begging me to stop.

I wouldn't stop.

I'd haul her onto her knees and sink into her, taunting her with how wet she is for me. I'd lean over her, pressing my hips into her sore bottom—make her remember who is in charge—and whisper the Mayfair Rules of Order in her ear as my cock strokes her to her first orgasm.

No Drama, No Sharing, No Exceptions.

I've learned the hard way that sex and love are fucking complicated. I play within the rules now for a reason. It's smarter. It's safer. And while I'm not normally a jealous man, when I think of Alison with someone else, my chest tightens. So yeah, if we were to hook up, I'd need us to be exclusive.

But still no strings.

Never said I wasn't an asshole.

Once you've been tied down and had your head messed with, though, you get wary.

Which isn't Alison's problem. None of my fucked-up issues are her problem, which is why I keep as much distance as possible.

Right now, that's about eighteen inches between my cock and her ass, because she's stopped suddenly. I skid to a halt right behind her.

Too damn close for comfort. Her hair smells like jasmine and vanilla, and when she twists to the side, pulling her phone out of her purse, her skin looks dewy soft.

Too. Damn. Close.

She glances at the screen, then rolls her eyes and starts

walking again, totally unaware of the fact that I'm gagging for another scent of her golden-brown waves. "Hailey's phone is fixed," she throws over her shoulder at me. "They're heading back to the hotel."

We're staying at The Grand, in a suite. I have a sinking feeling Cole's already arranged for another set of rooms for himself and Hailey.

The last thing Alison and I need is to be alone in a hotel suite together.

Fuck me.

I'm not an idiot. I see how she looks at me.

It can't happen.

That image of her, naked and on all fours for me, flashes through my head again.

And I'm back to swinging the shopping bags in front of my body. I don't know why my dick ever bothers going down. Might as well just stay hard all the time—it's an inevitable state around her.

She ducks her head as we approach the hotel. I don't see any paparazzi around, and they haven't bothered the girls yet this trip, but it's a reflex she's honed over the last two years.

Her family has done a fucking number on her head, that's for sure. I almost feel sorry for her, before I remember that she's one of the richest twenty-year-olds in the country and if she wanted to stay out of the limelight, she could.

There's something about Alison that's attracted to the fire. She's the youngest of four, and on paper, most definitely a good girl.

Straight-A student. Not a party girl.

Not a wild child hippie like her sister, who's a rebel in her own way. I grin to myself as we cross the lobby. I like Hailey a lot. She pisses me off when she ditches me, but she doesn't do that much anymore. We've come to an understanding.

Her baby sister, on the other hand?

No, there's no hope for Alison and me to ever come to an understanding. Not unless she is naked and turned over my knee.

As if she can sense my spanking fantasy, she turns and looks at me. "What?" she asks, her sculpted brown eyebrows tugging close to each other.

"Nothing." I wait to smirk until she's moved past me onto the elevator. Too late, I catch her watching my reflection in the mirror.

She stares at me in the glass for a minute, then smiles, and the feline power there makes my balls pull tight. "Right. Nothing."

———

Four hours later, I'm sitting at the bar in a trendy New York restaurant, watching Alison taste the first pour of a bottle of wine. She rolls it around in her mouth, then gives the sommelier a smile so full of grace it fucking hurts, and he gives a slight bow before filling the rest of her glass and that of her sister.

It's probably a two-hundred dollar bottle of wine and everyone here will bow and scrape to pour it for her.

She's the epitome of a spoiled little rich girl who gets everything she wants. Well, most of the time. I denied her my forced attendance at her birthday dinner. It was an asshole move, but necessary for self-preservation. Cole had begged off of dinner, which gave me an excuse to sit across the restaurant instead of right next to her. "Enjoy your dinner with your sister," I'd said, and Hailey had given me a knowing look as she'd pushed Alison toward their table.

We aren't fucking subtle, that's for sure. Ten months we've been circling each other, Ms. Reid and I.

Ten months I've been jerking off to the barely-legal fantasy of her on her knees, me teaching her how to suck my cock just the way I like it.

Ten months I've been punishing myself for being such a fucking pervert. Doesn't stop me from doing it again the next night. Or morning. That first moment of consciousness when I imagine her sliding down my body, licking my abs as she makes her way to my cock...

I groan and rub my jaw.

"Tough day?"

I glance up.

The bartender—pretty, young, *interested*—is smiling at me. She's got straight black hair and bright blue eyes. This is a classy place, so she's covered from the neck down, but it's all tight black fabric, and she knows how to stand to show off what she's got.

It's meant to be tempting.

I'm not dead, so it works, but just for a second. "I'll take another of these." I point at my ginger ale. "I'm working."

"Sure thing." She straightens up, her smile shifting from seductive to helpful. "Let me know if you need anything."

First thing I learned when I came back from London was that "I'm working" was universal code for "I'm a cop." Which I'm not, but since it's a made-up, imaginary code invented by bartenders to make sense of a guy like me not drinking in a place like this, I use it to my advantage.

In England, everyone assumed I was either a wealthy American businessman or a spy. That was convenient, because both were true.

And then neither was true, and my life fell apart.

But I pulled myself out of the gutter and now I'm here—watching Alison Dashford Reid cross her legs in that too-short dress for the waiter. I'd say I'm being punished, but other than wanting to bodily move that guy out of the way and enjoy the flash of her thighs for myself, I can't honestly call this penance.

She's why I've stuck with The Horus Group for nearly a year.

And she's why I'm going to have to walk away after this weekend.

[3]

ALISON

Dinner is fantastic. I feel like a million bucks and I have my sister's undivided attention.

So why do I care that Scott's being all chatty with the bartender?

I don't care.

Liar.

Okay, I do care. I don't understand why he won't touch me. I don't understand why I can't get over that. I've obviously turned him into some kind of romantic hero in my head. My psychology prof would have a field day with this mess.

It would get even worse if I told her about my mother.

"What are you thinking about?" Hailey frowns at me.

"Nothing." Definitely not the fact that our mother probably has an inappropriate relationship with our grandfather, and I've known that long enough that it's scarred me emotionally, and so far I haven't been able to bring myself to have sex with anyone. Nuh-uh. Not that.

"You're thinking about Scott."

Sort of. "Maybe."

"Last year, I was so worried he was going to take advantage of you, but now I think it's him that I need to worry about."

I stick my tongue out at her. "Your big, bad bodyguard can't protect himself?"

She laughs. "You're stubborn. I fear for anyone who gets on the wrong side of you."

"I'm the nicest."

"No, you're the smartest. I'm the nicest."

"That's true."

"Which makes Taylor the what?"

I scowl at Hailey. "Shush. Not on my birthday."

"Sorry."

"She sent me a text. Poolside on a rooftop somewhere. Santa Monica weather certainly beats New York this time of year. I might go visit her for Spring Break."

Hailey's eyes go super-wide. "No."

"It'll be fine."

Our older sister is a bit...reckless. She's a party girl, and has never met a scandal she hasn't wanted to get sticky in. This time last year, she was blowing the Vice President of the United States. And filming it, maybe.

She's never admitted that she was responsible for the home movie that was leaked of the two of them. But Taylor loves a good splash.

I can see Hailey's concern. The problem is, she's way under-estimating my ability to say no.

I'm not either of my sisters.

I'm not Taylor. I'm not a party girl, dangerously reckless in search of her next high.

But I'm also not Hailey, hungry for normalcy.

Secretly, I'm a mix of the two of them. I want that reckless release, I just want it in private and with the right man.

"It won't be fine..." Hailey starts to lecture. I take a big swallow of wine, bigger than is polite. She gives me a look. She usually doesn't let me drink out in public, but it's my birthday. I give her a little smile, and her look softens. "Anyway, I'd rather you didn't go anywhere on your break week, because...reasons."

"Of the wedding bell variety?"

She tips her head to the side. "Maybe."

"Okay."

"Okay? Just like that?"

I nod. I want to go out to L.A. and see Taylor, but it can wait. I know I'm going to be the only family member at Hailey and Cole's wedding. She hasn't been on speaking terms with our father since he maybe killed a call girl.

Cole had covered it up. That's what brought him into Hailey's life, and for six months, she'd hated him for it. Fair enough, right? But there was more to Cole, and The Horus Group, than just crisis management and security expertise.

The fact that Hailey had been kidnapped after Cole fell in love with her is probably proof of that.

I shudder as I think about how close I came to losing my best friend and the only other sane member of my family. "Just like that. I'd do anything for you, Hailey."

"Same, sweet pea."

"Even let me date Scott?"

She laughs. "No, not that."

I glance at the bar. He's stopped talking to the bartender. Good.

"Just as well. I don't want to date him anyway." She gives me an incredulous look and I stick my tongue out at her. "I don't. I just want him to..."

"God, that's even worse."

"Why?"

She gapes at me for a moment, then closes her mouth and

shrugs. "You're right. It's not. Do I need to give you a safe sex lecture?"

"No."

"Do I need to give you a safe heart lecture?"

God, no. "That's a definite no. I'm not romanticizing anything, Hail. I just want...It's time, you know?"

She winces. "Stay a kid forever."

"Can't. That's not how it works."

"Then be safe. Because a man like Scott—" She cuts herself off and takes a long, fortifying gulp of wine. *Like Cole*. "He can overwhelm you if you aren't careful."

"I'm not sure he'll be game for even a casual hook-up. He's done a bang-up job of ignoring my advances."

"Have you tried just being straight up with him?"

I blush. "What?"

She rolls her eyes. "Oh, Alison. Don't tell me you're trying to seduce him or something like that."

Maybe. I clear my throat. "What else...how else...you know. Help me out."

"If you play games, then he'll always be wondering what else is going on that he can't see. Strings, that kind of thing. But if you lay your cards on the table, then he'll do the same. And you'll both know—either this is a good idea, or it's not, and you can let it go once and for all."

"How..." Completely unsexy. Except what I think I really mean is *unromantic*, and isn't that the point? Romance has its place, like with Hailey and Cole, at least once they hooked up. "Was that what it was like with you and Cole?"

We talk about almost everything, but we've never talked about how she started dating the intense crisis management expert—a so-called Washington "fixer". Mostly because I assume it started with something super dirty, and I don't need that picture of my sweet-as-apple-pie older sister.

I already have images like that of my other sister, thanks to YouTube, and my mother, thanks to my vivid imagination and too-thin walls at my grandfather's estate.

Making a face, I reach for my wine. "Never mind. Don't answer that."

Hailey laughs. "It was different with us, because it's different for everyone. And we had strong feelings from the very beginning, so there was a lot of resistance to that. I was terrified of what having a crush on Cole would mean for me, that he'd suck me back into his world, and all I wanted to do was escape it."

Instead, she'd pulled Cole out of it. He wasn't exactly a good guy now, but good-er. I giggle, then realize I'm way too much in my head and nod more soberly. "Sorry. Yes. Right."

"No more wine."

"Of course not." I reach for the bottle. She doesn't stop me. I want to look over at the bar again, but I don't. I pour myself another glass instead.

"He's watching you."

I don't smile at that. It's good, but it's not great, because I don't know what to do about that information.

"What do you want from him?"

"Sex," I say immediately.

She winces, but then takes my glass out of my hand and empties it in one swallow. "Then go get it, birthday girl."

"Yeah?"

She opens her purse and pulls out her phone. "I'm calling Cole. The suite is yours for the night. Don't get hurt."

"Your bodyguard isn't going to hurt me." Not even if I beg him to.

"Right. Don't hurt him, then."

"I'm harmless."

She smirks and tips her head in his direction. I take a deep breath and stand up. By the time I turn around, he's standing, too.

There's nothing else in my line of sight, just a tall, broad, dark haired man in a suit that fits him like a glove. The carefully designed lighting highlights his few days of stubble that looks like it was perfectly groomed like that, but I know it's not, because I've watched it grow in.

My heart pounds in my chest.

I've been watching this man for ages. I know what he likes—my ass—and what he hates—my age, my family, my wealth, my presumed immaturity, although that last point isn't really fair.

But he doesn't know that.

So this is like high noon at the O.K. Corral, because we're going to do this. One last show-down.

Not really the way a one-night stand should start. I shake my hair out and try to smile, but I'm nervous.

Hailey's gotten my hopes up. *Tell him what you want.* Just like that, and she thinks it'll work.

I think she's insane.

But I'm genetically designed for bat-shit crazy. I've got this.

[4]

SCOTT

ALISON IS NERVOUS. Fuck me, she's *nervous*.

I can handle her brassy. I can handle her coy. I can handle her waving lace panties in my face and promising she'll wear them for me later.

I can't handle her like this, raw and real and exposed.

It's not fair, because I'm locked tight behind layers of lies, and she's just shown me a sliver of herself straight through to her soul.

I don't think of her as a kid. Not at all. She's a woman, through and through, but she's a young one, and right now, she's wearing her heart on her sleeve.

I'm going to break her heart, and it's going to hurt.

That little black dress swings around her hips and her hair bounces around her shoulders as she makes her way over to me. The whole picture is the definition of temptation. Long, smooth legs. Black heels. Bright eyes and lips with just a hint of shiny colour. Enough that my eyes are drawn to her mouth, but a promise that when I kiss her, all I'll taste is eager, ready woman.

If. Not *when* I kiss her.

And not if, either.

I'm not going to kiss her.

Keep telling yourself that, Mayfair. I take a deep breath and shove my hands in my pockets to keep from pulling her close to me.

"Hailey's calling Cole," she says as she stops in front of me. Even with her in those gorgeous heels, I'm tall enough that I'm looking down at her. She's small enough that she needs to tip her face up to talk to me, exposing that long stretch of creamy skin from her heart-shaped face down to her—

First step in not kissing her would be not looking at her perfect tits and the intoxicating shadow between them in the cleavage created by that bra she teased me with earlier, and the dress that, upon closer inspection, looks like it's offering her breasts up for a taste.

Second step would probably be not inspecting her God damned dress.

I nod and glance over her shoulder. "I'll wait until he arrives, then I can escort you wherever you want to go next."

A small smile twists at her lips. "Do you..." She trails off, then squares her shoulders. The nerves flee her face. She may be young and innocent, but she's strong as steel at her core. "I want a cupcake."

I don't know what I was expecting her to say. That wasn't it. "A cupcake? That's all?"

She grins, her eyes crinkling, and she shakes her head. "Nope. That's not all. But that's what I want first. Can we do that?"

I glance back at her sister. Cole's walking in the door behind Hailey. We make eye contact, and I nod, first at him, handing over his fiancée to his care, then again down at her little sister. "Yeah. We can get you a birthday cupcake."

We hit a late-night bakery two blocks away, halfway back to the hotel, and end up buying a six pack because Alison can't decide what she wants. At first it was lemon meringue, then chocolate raspberry, then vanilla bean... finally I just cut her off.

"We'll take those four that she mentioned, and two of those Death by Chocolate ones."

The girl behind the counter winks at Alison. "Your boyfriend likes chocolate, huh?"

Alison laughs and throws me a saucy look. "He's not my boyfriend," she says, her eyes dancing. "He's just my booty call. I'm feeding him to be polite."

I growl at her, which both women take as foreplay, and maybe it is. I hand over my credit card. "It's her birthday. She's not feeding me, it's the other way round."

"So that was the only part of my statement you felt the need to dispute? Who was feeding whom?" Ali asks as we step back into the cold night.

I look at the cashmere wrap she's holding tight around her body. "Are you warm enough?"

"No," she says baldly. "But it's not much further now."

I stop and take off my jacket and sling it around her body. I'm not carrying my handgun this weekend, so I don't need to keep the jacket on, and two blocks of her shivering will just about kill me. "Come on, let's get you back to the hotel."

"But I need a coffee to go with the cupcakes," she says with an innocent look.

"I know what you're doing," I mutter, steering her into Starbucks.

"What am I doing?"

"You're turning this into a date."

She laughs. "This is the world's worst date. I promise that's not what I'm doing."

I snort.

"You don't believe me."

I shake my head.

"Fine," she says, her voice still dancing with laughter. "But for the record, you have zero imagination if *forced date* is the only explanation you can come up with. And that doesn't speak very highly of me, either, that I need to manipulate you into spending time with me on my birthday."

"You don't need to—"

She cuts me off. "I honestly just want a cupcake and coffee. For real." She steps around a display of coffee beans, pauses for a second to admire a Valentine's themed takeout mug on sale, then moves to the cash, where she orders a vanilla latte. "And..." She glances back at me. "A dark roast, black, for my friend here."

I lift one eyebrow at her.

"What? I just assumed you wanted a boring old-man coffee."

I laugh out loud, because that's honest-to-God the funniest thing I've heard all day. Given that I've spent most of the day growling and fuming and worrying about her and her sister, that's not saying much, but I still appreciate it nonetheless. "Yeah, okay."

She smirks at me as we move to the far end of the coffee bar and wait for her order. Mine is good to go immediately. And she's not wrong, I do prefer drip coffee—just with lots of cream and sugar in it. Which conveniently, I can fix myself while she's waiting.

She waits until I set my cup back down on the bar next to her hand before telling me, casually as can be, what else she wants for her birthday. "After we eat the cupcakes, I'm going to suggest we have sex. Again. I mean, I'm going to suggest it again." She turns to the barista who is about to hand Ali her latte and adds, totally unnecessarily, "We haven't had sex yet, of course. It wouldn't be *sex* again. I imagine once I wear down his defences, I won't have to make such a big production about it the second, third, and twentieth times."

She leaves me standing there, speechless, as she takes her latte with a grateful smile and goes to find a lid for it.

Fuck. Me.

"This was a trap," I mutter under my breath as I hold the door for her. As soon as we get back to the hotel, I'm leaving her with her cupcakes and barricading myself in my room.

Except it's her birthday and those are her birthday cupcakes and...Fuck. Me.

"It's not a trap," she whispers. "It's me being ballsy and just saying what I want."

"You weren't being ballsy earlier when you dangled panties in my face?"

"Apparently not ballsy enough. That was more...teasing. Hailey said I should just tell you what I want. No games. So I want coffee and cupcakes, check, and then we can talk about what kind of sex we should have."

Jesus. "We're not going to have sex." Even as I say that, my balls ache at the thought of getting naked together. Tasting every last inch of her and burying myself deep in her body.

"You've got the wrong idea about me, you know."

"I do?"

"I'm not romanticizing you."

"Good. I'm not a romantic guy."

"I just want sex. Nothing else."

I want to tell her that there are a million guys out there that could help her with that problem, no strings attached, no drama, but the words die in my mouth. I grunt instead, a neolithic sound that should turn her off if for no other reason than it reveals me to be an idiot incapable of speech.

"Literally, just a booty call."

"No." We're at the hotel now, and I hold up the cupcake

travel box as we head into the lobby. "And not another word, or I'm withholding your treats."

She gasps, her eyes twinkling, and she presses her lips together.

She keeps that promise of silence the whole way up in the elevator. I hand her the cupcakes when we get to the room, and pull out the keycard. She knows the protocol now. She's supposed to stand at the door while I do a quick sweep of the space.

Instead, she follows me through the suite. She sets her coffee next to mine on the tray on the leather ottoman, drops my jacket on the couch and her wrap on the floor, then trails after me into her room, where she kicks off her heels.

I ignore the desperate, horny thud in my groin at the sight of her bare feet—feet, for fuck's sake, but they're gorgeous, and that's like her third step to naked. I stalk back to the living room space and wait for her to follow, because I'm not leaving her in her room, which is a trapped space, until I've verified the entire suite is safe.

She smiles as we clear my room, and she's practically vibrating by the time I check the closet and the balcony and declare it safe for her to go to bed.

She doesn't go to bed.

Instead, she throws herself onto the couch and pats the cushion beside her. I grab the cupcakes and set them on the couch between us.

She picks up the lemon one and swipes some of the icing with the tip of her tongue.

When I don't react, at least not outwardly, she rolls her eyes and proceeds to eat the rest of the cupcake in the most delicate way possible. A swipe of icing, then a nibble of cake. Not a crumb falls as she consumes it, and my cock thickens as my brain readily transcribes what I'm seeing in front of me into an

X-rated fantasy of Ali on her knees in front of me, lapping at my throbbing dick.

I shift in place and her gaze drops to my lap.

Aw, hell.

I cross my legs.

She laughs.

This is not happening. I grab one of the two chocolate cupcakes—I don't count the raspberry one, because fruit has no place in a chocolate cupcake—and I peel back the wrapper.

I am not capable of eating it daintily. A crumb falls on my tie and before I get it, she's leaning over the cupcake box and snagging it for herself.

"Yummy," she whispers as she licks it off her finger.

"Stop it."

"Make me." She winks.

I stare her down as I finish eating, then I reach for my coffee. The staring contest continues as we finish our drinks, then I sit back and sigh. "Fine, you've got my full attention. Why me?"

"You're hot."

"Try harder."

"You're a good guy." Not even a little bit. I snort, but she waves me off. "I've been watching you. You're good with Hailey —you get her. You see our fucked-up family and how screwed up our relationships are and you help smooth it over for her when she needs to bounce, or not show up at all."

"That's the job."

She shakes her head. "No. I've grown up around guys like you. Everyone has an angle. Nobody just does the job, no questions asked."

That makes me so mad at her father, who is a grade-A scum, and her mother, who has no moral compass that I am aware of. "They should."

"They don't. But you do." She holds my gaze, daring me to

tell her she's wrong. She's not, because yeah, I'm good at my job. She licks her lips. "And you want me."

"No—"

"Don't deny it, not on my birthday. You want me," she repeats in a quick, staccato burst of nerves. "And you are a good guy, and I want this. I want you to have sex with me, because you're a good guy and you're hot and you want me. I want you too, in case that wasn't clear. But just for sex. I'm not—"

"Whoa. Slow down." If I ever thought Hailey was the earnest one, it was only because I hadn't had a conversation like this with Ali yet.

A dangerous, addictive conversation where her eyes are bright and her chest is rising and falling and her words have me so hard it hurts.

I don't want to like her. I don't want to think of her as Ali or know that she's lonely.

I definitely don't want to be a red-blooded man with the knowledge that she's turned on and willing—eager, even—but picky.

And she's picked me because she thinks I'm a good guy.

"I do want you. Any man would, and I'm flattered that you think I'm good enough for you. But you don't really know me, and if you did, you wouldn't want me. I'm not the guy you think I am."

"Okay, scratch the good guy stuff. I don't think the details of that matter for a one-night stand. What matters is that you wouldn't kiss-and-tell, that I can trust you not to hurt me, that you'll wear a condom, that kind of thing."

"That's not being a good guy, Ali, that's just...Jesus, don't have sex with anyone...fuck that, don't have *lunch* with anyone who doesn't think those are the most basic ground rules."

"I haven't."

"Good." I glare at her. "But the answer is still no."

Her lower lip stiffens and she drops her gaze to the cupcakes. Silently, she closes up the box and stands, carrying them to the small kitchenette near the window.

I stand as well. "It's not that I don't want to," I offer lamely. "You're gorgeous."

She doesn't say anything.

When I was a SEAL, we practiced surviving torture techniques way more complicated than the silent treatment from a beautiful woman. Even Maddie never successfully managed to guilt me by giving me the cold shoulder.

But tonight—fuck, it's her birthday. And I'm breaking her heart. I stand in the middle of the room, ready to take the hits when she turns around. I deserve them.

"You break every single one of my rules," I say quietly. "And I definitely don't seduce women young enough to be my—"

She whirls around. "I am *not*... whatever you were about to say, I am not that much younger than you."

"I'm thirty-four."

She blinks at me. "Well...okay. You're older than I thought. I won't hold that against you."

"That doesn't mean that *I* can't hold it against me. And I would. I do. There's no part of me that isn't anxious about the fact that you're twenty."

She looks at my dick again. Fine. There's one part that has zero problem with the fact that she's barely legal. He twitches. More than okay with that fact.

"Another reason this is against the rules," I say drily. "I'm a dirty old man."

"I gotta say, banging my sister's bodyguard is part of the appeal. So if you keep underlining the forbidden aspect of why we can't, that's just going to convince me that we should."

"I'm not convincing you of anything. I'm just stating how it is." To show her that I'm not getting into a confrontation over it, and that I'm totally fine with drawing that boundary—and no, I don't need to run away to my room like a scared little boy—I take the armchair, which seems wise until she sighs and moves closer.

I walked right into that trap. Cole and Jason would be howling at me right now, because I'm cornered between a determined, sexy woman and the wall. Rookie mistake, and I'm no rookie.

"You've got rules," she whispers, her lips twisting in a smirk. "And you think I can't play within them?"

Alarm bells clang inside my head. "Something like that."

"You wanna tell me what these rules are?"

"Nope. I want you to go to bed."

"Tuck me in."

"Not going to happen."

"It's my birthday."

I need to get up and walk away from her. I try. I stand up, and she moves back. I need to walk past her and into my own room, tell her I'll see her in the morning and close the door. But then she sighs and turns around, her long, honey-brown waves spilling down her back as she glances at me over her shoulder.

"If you won't come tuck me in, the least you could do is unzip my dress." She walks a few feet away from me, giving me lots of space.

I clear my throat. "You got into it, you can get yourself out of it."

"I had Hailey's help, actually. But okay. Hmmm." She twists her arms behind her back—fuck, how is she that bendy? This is not good for my control. Her fingertips snag her zipper and she tugs, revealing a widening triangle of skin. Not the bra she flaunted earlier.

No bra at all.

Fuck me, because now all I can think about is the question, is she wearing those panties?

Is she wearing *anything* under that dress?

"Don't jerk me around, Ali." My voice is strained. I'm close to snapping. I don't want her to know it's really that I'm close to *breaking,* so I let her think I'm straight-up angry about the tease.

Truth is, I'm not sure she realizes just how far she's pushing me. Something she said earlier has been bugging me.

Here's to another year of bodyguard-enforced virginity.

She's hot as fuck, and she's been in college for almost three years.

No way is she still a virgin.

I haven't.

"I'm not..." She sighs and turns around, and she's gorgeous and sexy and totally innocent as she gives me a helpless little shoulder shrug. "Okay. I guess I'm pushing you hard. I'm sorry."

God damn it. I scrub my hand over my face. "I don't get involved with clients, or the family of clients. I don't do high-profile relationships. I don't have one-night stands." The words drill out of me, slamming against her. "And those are just three of the reasons why this can't happen. What else? Did you think about what happens when you wake up from this hormone-driven fun-fest?"

Her face slacks. She looks stricken. I'm an asshole.

"Maybe you aren't thinking of the consequences. Maybe you can't imagine them yet, but there are adult—"

"Stop calling me a child."

"Stop acting like one." I sigh as that hangs between us, harsher than it needs to be. And it's not really true. "I'm the last person to romanticize sex, believe me, but—"

"Then don't," she says, crossing her arms over her chest. Her dress is still unzipped behind her, and the straps are all loose and wobbly. I watch as one shifts to the outer edge of her shoulder. Another blithe shrug and it would drop down her arm, baring the top of her breast. "Don't romanticize anything. Clearly I haven't done a good enough job of making it clear that I'm just looking for a safe hook-up."

"I told you. I don't do casual hook-ups, so you're out of luck."

She frowns, her lower lip plumping out in a way that says, *taste me, asshole. Taste me and then tell me you don't want me.* "What *do* you do?"

"All due respect, Ms. Reid, that's not really your business."

"Your hard-on says it is." She recrosses her arms, loosening her hold on her dress. It slips a bit.

"He's a liar." *Go to bed,* I growl in my head, but somehow it doesn't come out like I want it to. It doesn't come out at all. I look away because I can't stop staring at that bare bit of her chest, hungry for more. "And we need to stop talking about sex."

"I would've thought your rule was that you always had to be in charge," she whispered, and I snap my head back to her. Her words pull me closer. I can barely hear her, and I swear she drops her voice as I get within touching distance. I'm losing this battle, I realize with a start. I've been having this whole conversation thinking I've got a handle on the situation, but right now? I'm right where she wants me.

And fuck it all, I'm right where I want me, too.

I *want* her. I'm not going to let myself have her, of course, but I'm lying to us both if I pretend I want her to go to bed.

I want her to drop that dress and then come over here and climb me like a tree. I want her in my arms, hot and needy and innocent and wet...

I'm closer again. But I don't touch her.

I'm not *going* to touch her.

I grasp for...something, anything. What comes out is

completely wrong. It's like I'm watching myself swallow the hook. "That goes without saying."

"That you'd be in charge?" she asks, her voice breathy and seductive. "And that it would be good, as long as I do what I'm told?"

"You wanna play some kind of Lolita game, Ali?" As soon as the words are out of my mouth, I know it's even more the wrong thing to say. Way worse, really, because instead of letting myself be reeled in, I've yanked too hard on the rod. I wanted to stop this, and now I have, by insulting her.

She stiffens, her shoulder blades pulling tight as if she regrets giving me that slice of her bare back. The temperature in the room drops ten degrees.

She glares at me. "I'm a twenty-year-old woman and it's my birthday. I don't know what your problem is, but that I'm young and sexy can't be it. And I don't fetishize myself, you asshole. I won't be shamed for hitting on you when I'm not doing anything wrong."

I don't have a good answer to that. But I can't stand here and say nothing, so I offer, again, the lame truth. "We can't happen."

"Fine. I apologize for wanting in your pants." When she goes to turn, it's slow, like she doesn't want to give me that slice of her back again.

I should accept it. I should let her go.

I shouldn't cross the space between us and slide my hand around her arm, spinning her back against me.

I shouldn't stare into her eyes and wonder how the hell I held out so long. Definitely shouldn't lower my mouth to hers and kiss her.

But that's exactly what I do.

And it's fucking worth it.

[5]

ALISON

I'M STILL THINKING he's going to chide me and send me to bed like a petulant child when he pulls me into his arms and his mouth comes down on mine. His hands slide into my hair and hold my head in place as he kisses me hard, then soft, then hard again when I whimper and open for him.

All I can think is, "Oh my God, he smells so good," and then, "Wow, he tastes even better," before my heart is racing too fast for individual thoughts to make sense.

The testiness of our...fight? Was it a fight? It was something, and it was ugly, but it's all gone now. Poof. Because Scott's kissing me like I've wanted him to for months. *Months*. His tongue is teasing mine, his lips are softer than I'd imagined, and so much better for it, and his hands are *everywhere*.

He squeezes my hips first, then my waist, and then—

I gasp into his mouth as his palm covers my breast through the loose fabric of my dress, his thumb finding my nipple with unerring confidence.

He freezes, and that just won't do. I wind my arms around his neck and push up onto my toes, pressing my flesh into his hand at the same time, and he kisses me again, deeper this time.

Yes, yes, yes please.

His mouth is hot and tastes like chocolate. His tongue slides against mine again, deeper, faster, and with each stroke he lights something dangerous inside me. Something that, once it gets burning, I'm pretty sure is going to be unstoppable.

Light me up, I think. *Light me up and let me fly, because I'm so ready for you*. I've been a good girl for so long. All my friends did this years ago, and do it regularly. But I waited until I was sure I was ready—although maybe nothing could have prepared me for this. But I waited until I knew clearly what losing control was like.

It made me a little mad that Scott thought maybe I didn't know what the consequences of this would be.

I probably know better than he does, but I don't need to tell him all the filthy family secrets just to hook-up with him. Since he's Hailey's bodyguard, he probably already knows, anyway.

Now that prickly defensiveness is fuel on the fire inside me. He didn't think I was ready, but now he's kissing me, and touching me, and *oh yes*, I'm ready.

Against my belly, I can feel his erection. On my chest, his fingertips have found bare skin, and he's tugging down my dress.

I'm ready, and he's—

Stopping.

This time, when he freezes it's not for a second. He doesn't kiss me again, no matter how close I press myself against him.

He holds me tight, but his mouth is buried in my hair now, and he's...I can feel him locking himself down. It starts in his arms, a tightening that moves to his core. All the muscles contracting, until the only part of his body that is still good-to-go is his dick, and he's proven time and again that he's willing to disappoint both me and his cock, so I'm not holding out any hope for that part of him to convince the rest to get back in the kissing-and-more game.

"You're a frustrating woman," he whispers roughly.

"So you do think of me as a woman," I sigh. Well, that's a bittersweet victory.

He huffs at that, then we stand there, hugging for another long moment before he finally says quietly, "Key takeaway is that you're frustrating."

"I beg to differ." I smile, because it's my birthday, and I got cupcakes and one hell of a kiss. I refuse to see this as a failure. Rome wasn't built in a day. "I take it you weren't planning on kissing me?"

"I was trying to explain why we can't happen, so...yeah. I wasn't planning on kissing you."

"But you did."

"I did."

"It was...hot."

His grip tightens around me for a second. "Unbelievably hot. If I were any other man..."

"And I were any other woman?"

"No. You're perfect just the way you are." His lips dust lightly over mine, then he deepens the kiss just long enough for his tongue to brush mine. My insides flutter at the angsty hope that we might do more, but he pulls back again.

"Scott?"

He shakes his head. "I can't. And it's not because I don't want you. But I won't like myself in the morning, and neither will you."

"I will. How many times do I have to tell you, I'm not asking for more than one night?"

His mouth tightens into a firm line. "I'm done with The Horus Group. This weekend is my last protecting Hailey." What? I shrink back from him, first inside the circle of his arms, then he lets me go. "I should have told you earlier."

I can't look at him. I wouldn't be able to look at myself,

either, so it's good that there aren't any mirrors in my line of sight. I'm such a hypocrite. I stare over his shoulder, willing the floor to open up and swallow me whole, because I don't want him to see me reacting like this. Like anything. *I'm fine with that.* I push as much indifference into my voice as I can. "Thank you for telling me before..."

He lets me trail that off. We both know what I mean. He nods gruffly. "Now you understand."

No. I don't. Because I still want him, still miss his mouth on mine and his arms around me. Even if it would have just been for one night, I wanted to have him.

And now he's fading out of my life, which is his right. He was never mine to begin with.

"Go back to school, Ali. Find a nice guy who worships the ground you walk on, who will make you feel like a goddess and keep you safe."

I huff a laugh, because the only man I trust to keep me safe is standing right in front of me. Too bad he doesn't meet the first two criteria. "Pipe dream."

"It's not." His voice is rougher than sandpaper as he stares at me. "You haven't given it a try, have you? Have you even dated anyone your own age?"

No. I clench my jaw and stare at him. "I think you made it clear that your sex life wasn't my business. So...ditto. None of your business, Mr. Mayfair."

He shoves his hands in his pockets. Tension is vibrating off him. "Why haven't you?"

"Because I couldn't!" I yell, startling both of us. He moves closer and I shake my head at him. I don't need to be comforted. I exhale roughly. "You know how fucked up my family is. I never wanted to be like them. But I am, you know? I don't want to date some guy from school. So I guess the apple doesn't—"

"Stop it." He's closer again. Push. Pull. Yes. No. We're the worst kind of perpetual motion machine.

I nod. We definitely need to stop it. He's been saying it all night. I stumble backwards, moving around a barstool toward my room. "Yeah. Good night."

"Ali..."

"Don't." I shake my head. "Thank you for the cupcakes. And the kiss. The rest of it...I'm going to pretend it didn't happen, and I trust you will do the same."

His jaw flexes and his eyes glitter with frustration, but he doesn't say anything else. He just watches me back into my room.

I close the door with a touch more force than is necessary.

When I wake up in the morning, he's gone.

[6]

SCOTT

It's been four years since I last walked in the front doors of Mayfair Tower, the Manhattan home of Mayfair Enterprises.

I'd hoped to never do it again, but beggars can't be choosers. Since most of my bank accounts are still frozen by the British government, I'm living pay check to pay check. And I just quit my job.

Jeff's office is on the far side of two security checkpoints, so I can't just stroll in and say, "hey, little brother, how about hiring me?"

Instead, I have to give my name to the security guard, pretending I don't see three ways I could disarm him and take control of the lobby in five seconds flat.

Maybe the job I should be applying for is chief of security.

After talking to someone on the phone, the guard directs me to a waiting room at one end of the lobby. This has been renovated since I was here last.

Business must be good.

I snort. Of course business is good. My brother was on the cover of national newspapers last week. The stories weren't about Mayfair Enterprises, but there he was in the background of a picture of the President doing a tour of one of our factories.

Our factories. No, not mine.

I've never wanted a piece of this company.

"Mr. Mayfair?" I look up at a tall, pretty blonde in a dark blue suit waiting to escort me to see Jeff.

I've never wanted this, but now I need it. And if I'm willing to accept the strings attached, it'll open up the world for me again.

"Yes," I say, standing.

She holds out her hand. "I'm Alicia. The other Mr. Mayfair's executive assistant. Please follow me."

We shake. Her cool grip is strong and sure. Good for her.

She leads me past security, grabbing me a visitor's badge on the way. As we walk, she tells me that Jeff's currently on a conference call, but he's got lunch in thirty minutes, and would I like a sandwich?

It's quarter after eight in the morning. "I just had breakfast, but thank you."

She doesn't blink. "Mr. Mayfair's operating on UK time this week."

"Ah. So a late lunch, then."

She doesn't laugh. I swallow a sigh.

When we reach Jeff's office suite, she directs me to an empty office on the far side of her desk. "You can wait in there."

"Thanks." I walk past her, already feeling restless.

"And Mr. Mayfair?"

"Yeah?" I turn back and look at her.

"Your mail is waiting for you in there."

Jesus. I head in without acknowledging that further. Sure enough, there's a stack of what looks like annual reports on the desk, and a small pile of envelopes next to them.

Jeff didn't waste any time in laying the guilt trip.

My phone doesn't work in here—no surprise there—so I sit down heavily in the leather desk chair and flip through the letters first. Annual statements of accounts I don't have access to, with red stamps on them confirming that they're still locked because I'm a bad boy.

Or something like that.

My fucking father.

The start of a headache pinches between my eyes. I breathe deeply, slowly, locking that shit down. I'm not going to get sucked in. I don't need *that* money. The zeroes swim in front of my eyes. Shit, nobody needs that much money.

I just need Jeff to intervene on my behalf with the Brits, get my access to my own damn money, and then it can be another however many years before I need to be slammed in the face with the fact that I'm a terrible son.

"What are you doing here?"

I set down the report I'm reading and look up at my brother. Three years younger than me and infinitely smarter. Fewer qualms about the moral gray areas in life, too. "Apparently having lunch with you."

Jeff laughs. He's got my dark hair and eyes, but he's clean-shaven to my few days of scruff and leaner to my bulky mass. Not that he's not strong. He spent a few years training as an MMA fighter, but his strength in the ring is his speed, not the weight behind his fists. "Alicia explained I'm on London time?"

"What's that about?" I get right to it.

"We're building a nanotechnology research lab in Leeds."

"That's different."

He shrugs. "It's a test run. I'm trying to convince Mother it's a good direction to take the company."

"The British government hasn't given you any problems?"

"Because of you?" He gives me a look of surprise, as if to say, *you think you're that important?*

"I'm still having some difficulties with them. Frozen bank accounts, a lot of red tape."

"The Company didn't bail you out?"

I laugh. "I wasn't a CIA operative."

"Sure. Of course not."

Not while I'd been in London, anyway. But I was recruited by the CIA after I left the Navy—after my very short stint here at Mayfair Enterprises failed miserably—and I'd been trained... Farm-adjacent, let's call it. "No, my former employer hasn't provided any assistance with restoring my access to my accounts. And I'm still on a travel ban."

Jeff frowns. "Really?"

"Dude, welcome to the common-man reality. Do you know how much red tape is involved with getting off a no-fly list?"

"That's what lawyers are for."

"I can't afford a lawyer."

"How poor are you at the moment?"

I've got five grand in my West Maryland Credit Union account, and I'm getting another paycheck from The Horus Group. I own my truck outright. But I don't have the tens of thousands it would cost to hire a lawyer to untangle the mess I left in the UK. Well, I don't have access to the funds. They're all locked up tight in England.

Fuckers.

"I'm not poor, exactly."

He gives me a confused look, and I resist the urge to punch him for being so privileged he didn't get it. He sighs. "Do you need a loan?"

"Fuck you. I need a job."

He points at the desk. "Whenever you want it."

Sharp, cold self-loathing crawls up my back. Never in a million years. "Not this kind of job. Something in the plant, maybe, or on your security team."

"Mother would have a coronary."

"We don't need to tell her."

"She'd find out." He leans against the door frame and rubs his jaw as he gives me an appraising look. "What's your plan, man?"

I don't have one. "It was to be a Navy SEAL for twenty-plus years and retire in Boca Raton, but Dad fucked that up for me, didn't he?"

"He just wanted you to take your rightful place."

"*Your* rightful place. And it looks good on you."

He shrugs. "I like it."

"You're living in another fucking time zone this week. You love it."

He grins. "I love that part. I love the thrill of a new project. But...change might be coming."

"What kind of change?"

He shakes his head. "Not here."

How mysterious. But I'm not getting sucked into his drama. "Taking over the world looks good on you. But it's not for me."

"So re-enlist."

"It's not that simple." What I did in England means that I'm probably ineligible, anyway.

"You were working with Cole Parker in Washington."

I give him a hard look. "Keeping tabs on me?"

"Was that a secret?"

"That's not an answer."

"Neither is that."

I want to get up and pace. Instead, I lean back in the leather chair and swing my feet onto the desk. "I'm not working with them any longer."

"Were you fired?"

"What the hell? No, I wasn't fired."

He spreads his hands wide. "You don't want the special

treatment. 'Just a job in a plant.' I'm not sure you'd pass the job interview, asshole."

I give him my middle finger and shove away from the desk. Pacing will have to do.

"As a matter of fact, I do have a job for you," he says quietly. "And if you do it, I'll see what I can do about freeing up your British bank accounts."

I don't like the tone he's shifted to. "Is it legal?"

He winces. "Don't ask questions you might not like the answers to. Come with me."

Booty Call

Ali and Scott

part two

Washington

[7]

ALISON

I'm back in Washington, studying at a little coffee shop just off-campus one night when I see Scott next. It's late, after eleven, and I'm sitting in the window. This big-ass black SUV pulls up across the street, which of course gets my attention, because this is a quiet residential neighborhood and that kind of car screams, "don't fuck with me, I'll drive over you."

Not really standard fare for Georgetown.

I'm so messed up, that turns me on a little. It's my dirty little secret. My sister would be horrified. She's lived through the real-life drama of good guys and bad guys, and doesn't think anything about it is hot.

Well, except for her bad-ass fiancé. She thinks Cole's pretty irresistible. I've been in their apartment when they duck into their room for a private "conversation". It's embarrassing how much she digs his wickedness.

But I'm not one to judge.

Then Scott climbs out of the driver's side of the giant SUV I'm ogling.

He's in a suit, like always. No tie. Just a dark suit and a white shirt, muscles straining to be contained by fabric that's way too soft for him.

That turns me on, too, even as I start to slow-burn at the memory of how we left things between us.

I squirm in my chair and tug the hood of my sweatshirt up over my head. Why does the one guy that makes me want to give up my V-card have to be my sister's bodyguard?

Why can't I fall head-over-tits in lust for a football player or a kinky gamer boy?

You know why, a slimy little voice whispers in my head.

I sit up straight. No more squirming. And I'm making a therapy appointment as soon as I'm done studying.

But I don't look away from Scott. I watch as he glances around, then heads into the townhouse directly across from where I'm sitting.

I feel a momentary spasm of guilt for spying, but it's not like I sought him out. I was just sitting here, minding my own business, when whatever weirdness he's up to just happened right in front of me.

I'm completely legit to just sit here and see things.

Which is why I angle my chair away from the window, turn my computer just so, and turn on the camera so I can keep watching him.

Because I'm totally legit. Yeah, right.

My messenger app beeps at me. My friend Corey from the pre-law group wants to know if I'm up for a breakfast study circle.

A: Sure, what time? Can I bring...

I look at the display counter. They have lots of muffins left, and I bet they'll give them to me at half-price when they close in half an hour.

A: Muffins?

C: You can bring me muffins any time ;)

A: Ew.

C: Sorry. 9:30? McAllister Lounge?

A: Sure. I gotta be done at eleven, have a family thing.

C: Can't make a joke here about how it pains me to be quick?

A: You could if it would be funny. So... no.

C: I love you

A: I know

C: And a Star Wars reference. You're the perfect woman.

A: I'm really, really not. ;)

On the other half of the screen, the townhouse door opens, and Scott comes out.

A: Gotta go wash my hair. See you tomorrow.

I close out of both apps and make myself actually read my Poli Sci 407 paper. It's good, but it could be better. I get lost here and there in pretty words, a trait I've inherited from both of my parents. Ever since someone in the writing lab pointed it out in my first year, I've made it my mission to scrub all of that out of my assignments. It's one thing for an argument to shine on its merits. It's another to dress it up to look good, and I hate that with every fiber—

"Alison?"

I jerk my head up, shoving my computer a little as Scott surprises me. Didn't he get in his car?

Nope. He's standing right in front of me, and he kind of takes my breath away. Kind of? Ha, more like completely. He wears a suit unlike anyone else. And I'm surrounded by suits all the time. But he's *dynamic*, one minute looking like David Gandy on a GQ photo shoot, the next like the Incredible Hulk, ready to burst out of his clothes and take on the world.

But if he's really a monster, he keeps it under control.

There's no twenty-foot green rage machine here. Just a six-foot-plus man, but with a capital M.

Scott Mayfair is a Man, and I'm sitting here like a mute idiot, in sweatpants and a hoodie. I'm not even wearing a bra.

And while my brain is stuttering, failing to compute all of that holy unfairness, his obviously has no problem.

He gives me a concerned look. "What are you doing out so late?"

Oh, for fuck's sake. I'm obviously a college student, not a fucking child.

Clearly our last fight didn't make a strong enough impression, and *that* has me more pissed than anyone else. "I don't think that's any of your business," I say, and even though I meant it to be bitchy, the ice in my voice surprises me.

"You don't?" He gives me a look that I can't decipher. Part judgment, maybe part derision. I don't know. I don't like it.

"No, I don't. Last I checked, you don't work for The Horus Group anymore. And even if you did, I'm not one of their clients."

"You think my concern for you is professional?" His eyes glitter as he leans over. His right hand rests on the back of my chair. His thumb rubs against my shoulder and I can feel it through my sweatshirt. He puts his left hand on the table. He's right in my face now, and the look isn't mysterious anymore. He's mad.

At me.

For studying at eleven thirty at night.

What a fucking asshole.

So I laugh, because I was raised by assholes. Intimidation doesn't work on me. "What do you think you are you doing?"

"Clearing something up."

"And just what is that?"

"My concern for you is incredibly personal. My concern about you being out in the middle of the night is about how you get home, who you go home with, and what you do when you get there. The only answers I like to those questions are *safely*, *nobody*, and *nothing*."

"You don't want me to..." I blink up at him. He's close enough I can see the five o'clock shadow on his jaw and the corded muscles in his neck. "I'm not on a hot date here. Obviously."

"Why can't you study at home?"

"There are distractions at home. And why don't you sit down like a normal person while we have this conversation? Do you need to hulk over me like an oversized bulldog?"

He smirks and straightens up, adjusting his jacket—and his belt, which makes me wonder if anything else needs adjusting, too, but he sits down before I have a chance to check for an erection. He gives me an amused look as he settles into the chair. He's big and broad, taking up way too much space. One of his knees bumps the table from underneath. The other is dangerously close to rubbing against my leg.

"Here's the thing." I tap my finger against my lower lip as I give him a thoughtful look. It's all very deliberate, of course. After New York, I need to regain the upper hand.

With Scott, I'm perpetually off-balance. That just won't do.

"The thing?" He grins and leans in. He's playing with me, too. He knows how good he smells. The bastard.

"You were a jerk to me in New York."

He nods. "I was."

I watch his gaze drop to my mouth, which makes me think of kissing him. Does he know his mouth is tugged tight like that? Under tension, because he wants to lean in and kiss me, too?

Eyes up, Ali. "And now you're being all flirty."

He jerks his gaze up to meet mine. I gasp, just a little, a squeak of a noise, because yeah, he knows. Pure want burns in his eyes. I know the feeling. "I'm not," he growls.

"You *so* are. And you're a jerk to pretend otherwise."

"At least I'm consistent."

"Why?"

He shrugs.

Well, enough of this conversation, then. "Okay. I'm heading home."

"I'll drive you."

"Nope, I'm fine."

I shove my computer into my bag and stand up, making my way to the counter.

He follows, close enough to make the skin at the back of my neck prickle. I like it.

"You guys are closing at midnight, yeah?" I ask the girl at the counter. She nods. "Can I take the rest of the muffins off your hands?"

"Sure. I'll give them to you half-off."

"Thanks!" I say brightly. I ignore Scott while she bags them up, then I stow them in my bag on top of the computer and my notebook.

Then I head for the door. I don't get more than five feet down the sidewalk before his hand wraps around my jacket sleeve.

"Enough, Ali," he growls.

I blink at the bark. "Excuse me?"

"Come with me." He's pissed, and I should be—I don't

know, scared or something—but I'm not, because his hand grabs mine. *His fingers wrap around mine.* Scott's pulling me toward his car, and I'm probably grinning like an idiot.

"Are you going to punish me for being bad?"

"Jesus Christ, what the hell is wrong with you?"

"More than you could ever imagine."

"You're enjoying this."

"I have your full attention. Of course I'm enjoying this."

"What am I going to do with you?"

"Anything you want."

He jerks open the back door and gestures for my bag. I slide between him and the SUV and put it down on the back seat, then press against him.

"Stop that."

"Make me."

He laughs. "I'm more than you can handle."

"So you keep saying," I whisper.

His voice is low, but he doesn't stumble at all. It should scare me, how confident he is about sex. It doesn't. I can feel myself getting slick and he hasn't even said anything dirty yet. "You don't want me to turn you into my fuck toy."

Boom. Well, that was dirty. I try and fail not to blush. It might be true that I don't have any experience with being anyone's fuck toy, but while maybe I don't "Netflix and chill", I *watch* Netflix. I know that's not the only option.

Fuck him and his rules.

But mostly, just fuck him.

Preferably on my own terms.

"I've been thinking about that," I say, leaning in close enough that our noses almost bump. When you can feel someone hovering just above your skin and it makes you twitchy...I grin as Scott clenches his jaw. *Yes.* I've got him.

His legs bump against mine. His gaze burns on my skin.

"Don't you want to know what I've been thinking?"

"I'm not sure I do."

"Why not?"

"Honestly? I'm afraid if...when you tell me what it is, it's going to be something that I *can* live with."

I laugh. "Probably."

"Don't tell me."

"Why not?"

"Because I don't want to hurt you."

The echo of what Hailey had said a month earlier is too on-point. I snort. "Maybe I'll hurt you."

"Maybe." But his voice promises that he's been here, done this before, and he's pretty confident that he's an asshole.

That's fine. No reason I can't have a fling with an asshole. My heart is off-limits, and not just to Scott Mayfair.

"You don't work for my sister's fiancé anymore. And I'm not asking for a one-night stand anymore. Just a casual, no-strings attached continued flirtation. A secret flirtation, of course. And no...fucking. Not yet. Not until you're ready." I wink. It sounds perfect, and so does the helpless little grunt he makes in response.

I tap my fingers against his hard, broad chest. "What other rules did you have?"

"I honestly can't remember."

I grin. "Take me home, Scott. And the next time I'm out studying late, I'll be sure to let you know."

"That's your plan?"

"Do you want me to walk home alone? In the dark and cold?"

He groans. "Damn it."

I grin again. "One way or another, mister, you're going to end up on my speed dial."

[8]
SCOTT

A FEW DAYS LATER, I'm sitting in the lobby of the Maryland offices of Mayfair Enterprises, a sprawling campus of buildings filled with computer engineers and marketing staff. Unlike the New York headquarters, this place doesn't give me the heebie-jeebies, but I'm not sure why I'm here.

Jeff's favour was completely off the books, but he'd sent me a cryptic text message asking me to meet him here. The automatic doors slide open and in walks my brother.

Not Jeff.

Will Mayfair. Little brother. Fighter pilot.

I jump to my feet. "What are you doing here?"

He slowly pushes his aviator sunglasses onto his head and gives me a cocky smile. "I could ask you the same question."

"Jeff asked me to show. Shouldn't you be sunning yourself under a palm tree?" Will's the youngest of the three of us, and he's supposed to be out in California flying planes for the Air Force.

"Same deal. He asked me if I could make it out to D.C., and it just so happened there was a military transport I could hop on."

"He didn't send the jet?"

"He offered."

And Will wouldn't have wanted to owe Jeff—or our mother —anything. I get it. "You here long?"

He shook his head. "A few hours."

"Damn. Good to see you anyway." We exchange a bro hug and stay standing. "How's work?"

He grins broadly. "Fantastic. I'm deploying again soon."

I feel that familiar whirl of anxiety in my gut, jealousy and worry spinning together until the tangle is hard to see as two separate strands. I'll always miss the adrenaline rush of deployment. Nothing I've done since leaving the SEAL teams has even come close.

But he's my baby brother, so I also don't want him flying sorties over Iraq and Syria.

Of course, someone has to, and Will's one of the best.

I got yanked out of the service before I was ready. Doesn't mean I should deprive my brother of the same privilege to serve his country. I clap him on the shoulder. "Be safe."

"Always am."

Our moment is interrupted by a discreet cough from a familiar blonde in a dark suit. I don't miss Will checking out Alicia, and neither does she.

"Gentleman, if you'll follow me." She introduces herself to Will, and explains to me that Jeff had her fly to the area for a few days. We head through an open-concept computer lab to a room with blacked out windows. She presses a button on the table, which initiates a video call, and then excuses herself.

Will watches her go. It's a good view, but I don't have an appetite for cool and aloof these days.

When I took Ali home the other night, I gave her my number—in case she found herself out late again, I told her. Good excuse, anyway.

She used it the next morning to text me a selfie of her leaving for class and it made me smile for an hour. Wavy golden brown hair spilling out of a hoodie, a teasing wink...that's what does it for me now.

I just need to find a way to reconcile that with feeling like she's still off-limits.

But that would have to wait until after our mysterious summons, because the video call was flickering to life.

When the picture crystallized, though, it wasn't a call, exactly. It was a secure observation feed of a boardroom. It took a minute, and Will recognized it before me—fair enough, since I'd only been in it once before.

"That's the Mayfair boardroom in New York," he muttered beside me.

And it looked like the board meeting was about to begin. I didn't recognize everyone around the table, but could infer they were the board members. Our mother, chairwoman of the company, sat at the far end. Which meant that our video feed was coming from somewhere right in front of Jeff, probably.

What the hell was our brother up to?

The meeting started out totally boring. If we weren't scanning the video feed, looking for any tiny clue as to why we were quietly linked in to this meeting, what we were supposed to see, I'd probably have nodded off.

Previous minutes accepted.

Order of business approved.

Sales reports acknowledged and infrastructure spending debated.

Snore, snore, snore.

"The next item on the agenda is the matter of taking Mayfair Enterprises public..." Jeff said, the disembodied voice behind the secret camera.

What?

Our father's will was set up in such a way that while Will and I both inherited shares of Mayfair Enterprises, we don't get to vote with them unless we're full-time employees of the company. By proxy, our mother controls them. Which I've never cared about before, but what would happen if the company went public?

At the far end of the boardroom, Mother didn't look pleased. She also didn't say anything.

Jeff forges on, distributing a consultant's report about the details of a public offering. It means nothing to me, but the tension in the room is palpable.

Questions are asked by some of the board members, but by the time the meeting wraps up, I have no more clarity about what's going on than I did before the meeting started—other than the bombshell, of course.

Jeff wants to sell our company.

I don't know how I feel about that.

As the video feed broke off, the door swung open and Alicia stepped inside.

Obviously, she knows that we're here, and Jeff organized it... does she know what the board discussed? She must. It's not actually a secret.

I decide I don't care if I'm violating some secret. "What's going on?" I ask her.

She offers a polite smile. "Your brother thought you should know," she said as she let the door close behind her. "In case your mother tried to involve you in the discussion."

Beside me, Will crosses his arms. "She controls our shares. We don't need to be involved."

"Of course." Another polite smile. "If you'll just wait another moment or two, your brother should dial in for a private conversation."

Right on cue, the screen lights up again, and she punches in a code before leaving the room again.

This time, Jeff is front and center on the screen. He's back in his office, it looks like. "Will!" he booms. "You made it."

Our youngest brother gives him a raised eyebrow look. "What's with the cloak and dagger stuff? We couldn't have Skyped or something?"

Jeff laughs, but it's a fair question. It's entirely possible that our brother has lost objectivity when it comes to what's reasonable to ask of another human being.

I glower at him. "It's not funny. You inconvenienced me, and had Will fly across the country. For what?"

"I couldn't broadcast a regular stream, it had to be internal, and we don't have any facilities in California. If Will was getting on a plane, it might as well be to where you are, right?"

I guess. "All so we could hear first hand that you want to sell the company?"

"Take it public."

"What does that mean for us?"

He blinks into the camera. "You'd get your money."

"I don't want any strings-attached-cash, Jeff."

Beside me, Will nods. "We don't need your money."

"For one thing, it's *your* money, and speak for yourself, baby brother. Scott there has himself a cash flow problem. But that's not why I'm doing it." He sighs and rubs the back of his hand against his forehead. His perfectly tailored suit moves effortlessly with him, and I'm reminded that my brother is every inch the wealthy billionaire now. "I want to focus my attention on new projects, with my own venture capital. I don't want to report to a board and do what's best for a large company. So think of that what you will, but I want out, and since neither of you assholes are interested in stepping up..."

Ah. Fuck. I nod. "Okay, I get it. You don't want to continue to sit on the board and recruit a new CEO?"

"That would be an even longer, more drawn out process."

"And what if the board doesn't go for it?"

A shadow crosses his face, then he looks straight at us. "There are companies that would stage hostile takeovers. At the first rumors of board disagreement..."

"Is that what you want us to do? Leak the news?" Will shakes his head. "Don't involve us, man."

"No. God, no. But if you're approached...we should have a common response. United front."

Possibly against our mother. But I nod, because for all our differences, we're brothers, and we have each others' backs. "Okay."

We talk for a few more minutes, agreeing on what Will and I will say—deny—if we're approached by business reporters or representatives from other companies. Then Jeff signs off and we head back to the lobby.

I need to fill Will in on the papers Jeff had me re-appropriate from that Georgetown townhouse. Papers I documented carefully before couriering to him in New York.

"Do you have time to get coffee?"

Will gives a long, regretful look at Jeff's blonde assistant standing watch and nods. "I've got two hours before I need to be back at Reagan."

"Let's go."

An hour later, neither of us understand exactly why Jeff is so interested in mineral rights or nanotechnology, but we're in a hundred percent agreement that we don't want any part of it.

"It doesn't really impact on my life," Will says, shifting on the booth seat across from me in a run-down diner we found just off the interstate. "Do you think he'll want our help once he goes his own path?"

I shake my head. "Can you imagine the three of us trying to run a company? It would be a disaster. And you're deploying soon. Hopefully many more times before you're done flying. You don't need to think about this shit."

"And what about you?"

That was the million-dollar question. My phone vibrates in my pocket and I use that excuse to buy myself a second. Will laughs at me as I check the message and reply, probably too damn eagerly.

A: If I told you I was going to be studying late…

S: I'd give you a drive home.

A: In that case, I'm studying late tonight.

Something inside me shifts. I don't care about Jeff's crazy plans for nanotechnology or mining or anything else. I just want my brothers—both of them—to be happy and do whatever they want in life.

For the last four years, I haven't had that pleasure myself. At first, that was my father's doing. But now, I'm my own worst enemy. It's time for that to stop.

I look up at my brother. "I'm gonna try and live a normal life for the first time in forever."

Will gives me a disbelieving look, but I don't care. I'm already typing back a response.

S: Let me know when and where, and I'll be there.

[9]

ALISON

I IGNORE Hailey's busy-body stare. "I'm not telling you anything about Scott."

"He used to be my bodyguard."

"And now he's not." And I'm not telling her about what we're doing. Which isn't much. But I do have his phone number, and I use it, and it makes me happy. Even if all I use it for are nearly platonic late-night rides home.

She sighs. "You're my sister."

"That doesn't give you unrestricted access to my inner thoughts."

"Party-pooper."

"Go get your makeup done."

My sister's getting married today. It's a secret wedding of sorts—she only told me last week that it would be at a court-house here, and the date. I thought they might elope to Vegas, but this is more them.

We're getting ready at her place. Right now she's getting her make-up done, and I'm in her room, staring at her wedding dress. It's strapless and short, just to the knee, and it's perfect for the urban setting. We picked it out in February on our trip to

New York, and I love it more now than I did then—I'd wanted her to get something floatier, made of chiffon, but this is almost retro, with the stiffer silk.

I'm kind of overwhelmed by the fact that my sister is getting married today, but she's going to look like a million bucks when she does it.

"Your turn," Hailey says softly from behind me. I turn and look at her. Her hair is twisted in a princess-like updo and her makeup is flawless. Dark eyes, nearly nude lips with a touch of pink. She looks like a bride.

I want a minute alone with her. I smile. "Tell Tegan she can go next."

Hailey's friend from work is the only other person she's going to have at her wedding. My chest goes tight at the thought, and I reach out my hand and wiggle my fingers at her.

She joins me on the bed. "No making me cry now that I've got my makeup on."

"Okay." But I can already feel the tears welling up. I make my eyes as big and wide as they can go and think of multiplication tables. When that doesn't work, I get up and shove a few tissues into the secret pockets in my dress. Even if I can avoid the tears right now, when Cole actually puts a ring on Hailey's finger, I'm going to be a mess.

I look at her matching big eyes and grab a few tissues for her, too. I don't have many bridesmaid duties today, but making sure she has something to dab away the tears is one of them.

My other job is to make sure she's wearing something borrowed. I brought three things with me, because I wasn't sure what would be right. I dig the jewellery pouch out of my backpack and re-join her on her bed.

It's hard to have family heirlooms when your family is creepy and gross, but our grandmother had been a wonderful woman...I was pretty sure. She hadn't much liked our grandfather, which the more I discover about my family makes me think she must be a good person. At least a good judge of character.

I stifle a shudder at the thought of marrying and having children with such a bad person.

Like our own father. And mother.

I hold out the pouch. "Borrowed options."

"Oh!" She beams. "I hadn't even considered doing that. But it makes sense. And I've got blue panties on."

"Too much information."

She blows a raspberry at me and opens the pouch.

Inside is a strand of pearls from our grandmother, earrings of mine that I just really like, and a bracelet that Taylor gave me when I was nine. I explain each of them to her, and her fingers linger on the bracelet from Taylor, but finally she reaches for the pearls.

"Nana would like it if I wore these," she says quietly.

I let it go for now, and besides, those are the most bridal of the choices. And they match her lips perfectly.

Tegan knocks on the open door. Her blue-striped hair is styled in a way to show off the stripes perfectly, and her face is made up in a similar way to Hailey's. Funky elegance.

I'm digging this wedding.

"My turn?"

Tegan nods. "And then we can help the bride into her dress."

Hailey squeals, and I grin.

I'm not much of a romantic, but there is something super infectious about the love and excitement bouncing around this apartment. My step is light as air as I head to the stool to be made-up.

[10]

SCOTT

Love makes people crazy.

Even though I'm not working for The Horus Group anymore, Cole asked me to do him a solid on his wedding day. He'd followed his future mother-in-law out to Harpers Ferry earlier today, and now, while he gets married, he wants me to keep track of her.

Crazy.

On the other hand, it's the second time the small town in West Virginia has hit my radar this month. So I can sit on Amelia Dashford Reid for the afternoon, then go poking around an abandoned mine site that was referenced in the documents my brother had me steal for him.

Alison's not the only one with a crazy family.

I've already been inside the restaurant where Mrs. Reid is having a meeting in a private back room. I planted a listening device on the tray the waitress will take into the room. If I get lucky, she'll leave it in there. If not, I've got a heat monitor on the wall. I can see on my phone that the three people that started the meeting are still in there. It's not ideal, but it's what I can do with little notice.

While I'm waiting, I slouch lower in my seat and pull out my phone.

S: You heading to the courthouse soon?
A: Just getting made up. In lingerie, want to see?
S: Don't tempt me.
A: Can't help it. Seriously, I've tried.
S: Just the mental image is enough to wind me up, brat.
And I'm working.

Fuck, I'm so messed up over this girl. I don't know what I want, other than her, without any of the messy consequences of wanting her. My cake and eat it, too. Greedy bastard, I am.

A: Where are you?
S: On a job out in the country
A: Will you be back tonight?
S: Nah, probably not
A: I'll save my studying for tomorrow, then
S: No big wedding party?
A: Just a dinner. I'll be home before it's too late.

The invitation was a mile wide.
I wasn't going to take it.
Not tonight. Not after I spent the day stalking her mother, not on the day her sister got married.

S: Another night
A: Promises, promises
S: Oh, ye of little faith
A: I should have some faith?

S: Did I not say I was picturing you in lace and nothing else? Yeah, babe. Have some faith.

She sends a smiley face in response, and then goes radio silent. Her sister is getting married, after all. I can't hog her attention.

I return my attention to the heat signatures. There's some movement in the room, and the waitress hasn't even gone in yet. Crap.

The front door of the run-down building opens, and out walks an older, portly man I'd recognize anywhere. He'd been my covert boss for nearly three years.

If Cole wasn't getting married right now, I'd be getting his ass on the phone.

What the hell was Alison's mother doing meeting with the head of PRISM? The international black ops agency funded a lot of different organizations, including—until recently—The Horus Group, but nearly half its mandate was carried out by covert agents, trained by the CIA, and sent into the field completely on their own.

And then hung out to dry if and when their missions fail— an experience I've had first hand.

At least I wasn't assassinated. Something to be said for being relatively small potatoes in the world of international espionage.

I don't know what Cole's gotten wind of. I don't want any part of this, unless I need to be a part of this...Fuck.

I watch the director get in a car with a driver that I'd spotted when I arrived. It heads back in the direction of Washington. Amelia Dashford Reid comes out next, on the arm of a man I don't recognize. I snap photos, send them to Wilson, the hacker partner in The Horus Group, and set my truck in gear.

Wherever they go, I'll follow. And when I finally get home

tonight, I'll have the world's longest shower and wash off all of this grossness. This isn't the life I want anymore.

Ali.

Ali is all that I want now.

————

The next night, I'm the one who texts her.

S: Need a ride home tonight?

A: Always looking for a ride.

S: Bad girl.

A: Exactly.

And so it goes. I'm like a kid with a not-so-secret crush, but we're dancing around it, and she's okay with that. Each night we take a step toward actually calling what we're doing extended foreplay. And each night we stop a little short.

We've done this a few times now. Sometimes I find her. Sometimes she tells me she's out alone. I walk or drive her home, and leave her at her door because she's still working on wearing down my willpower, and I'm still working on what I want to happen next.

But there's no question that her texts make my day, every damn time.

And then on an unseasonably warm night in late March, she pushes the envelope a little further.

A: I'm going to be studying late tonight

S: Dashford Library?

A: Darkest corner of the campus... It's a nice night, but

I'll be so scared to walk home all by myself...

S: You want to walk?

A: If I have company

S: What time should I pick you up?

A: Midnight

S: That's some serious studying

A: I'm a serious girl

S: I have no doubt

A: Any chance I can turn this walk home into a booty call?

I don't answer her. I don't trust myself, either way. Yes, there's a chance. There's also a chance my inner moral compass will right itself and I'll leave this girl alone.

Not a good one, but there's always a chance.

[11]

ALISON

I'm wearing a dress tonight. It's this light cotton thing I found at the mall for twelve dollars. Hailey laughs at my love of the clearance rack, but every time I wear something like this, I feel a little more normal. And it's not like she's wrapping herself in Prada every day, either. But she hides her rich girl in a basket of wool that probably cost a few hundred dollars, easily. And she gives back to the community, too. But she also goes to black-tie things and...she fits in better, even if she doesn't like it.

The only trapping of wealth I cling to is my regular spa visit and my Agent Provocateur collection.

The rest of the time I'm wearing secondhand jeans and discount dresses, yoga pants and hoodies from Old Navy.

I eat ramen noodles and iceberg lettuce, too, now that I'm living on my own.

That was a big step, because I didn't want to get a job. Finishing my degree early...three more months to go now...was my biggest priority. I took an extra class each term, and summer school, and started my senior thesis halfway through my junior year.

And every time my faculty advisor gave me a doubting look

or a gentle reminder that everyone has limits, I buckled down and did my next task even better.

I'm on the Honor Roll. I spend less than four hundred dollars a month on groceries and clothes.

And I'm addicted to Scott Mayfair.

So right now, I'm wearing a dress.

Not because it's cheap. Not because it's surprisingly warm today.

No, I'm wearing a dress because when the spring wind swirls over my bare legs, the skirt's going to lift up. And I'm going to pretend to hold down the fabric, but not before Scott sees that I'm wearing barely there pink panties underneath.

A year ago, I would have said I had zero vices.

Now I'm seriously addicted to seducing an older man.

He finds me in the library. He shows up fifteen minutes early and lounges quietly in the chair across the table from me. He's overdressed for a midnight study session, in his dark suit and white shirt—I'm not sure the man owns jeans and t-shirts, and I find myself so distracted by that thought that I set aside my textbook and finally just look at him.

He's been looking at me for a while.

"Do you wear a suit every single day?" I finally ask him, breaking the heavy silence stringing between us.

"Most days," he says slowly.

"I like it."

"Good."

"I'm pretty much done here."

"I'm in no hurry." Half of his mouth lifts up in an almost-smile. "I like watching you work."

"I'd say the same to you, but I'm not sure what you're doing now."

His smirk deepens. "I'm trying to re-establish some business connections I had in England."

I laugh. "That's a total non-answer."

"Sure is."

I narrow my eyes at him as I tuck my laptop away and try to decide which books I want to check out and which can be re-shelved. "Here," I finally say, shoving most of them across the table at him. "Carry these downstairs for me."

"You need all these books?"

I shake my head. "But I've got the extra muscle tonight, so I might as well take them all and figure out which ones I need when I get home."

He follows me to the elevator. I walk in front of him a few feet, hoping he's checking out my legs, and when I turn around, his gaze is definitely tangled up in my lower body. I flush with inordinate pride, because how many times has he taken me home now and *not* given in to the need throbbing between us?

But I've got faith that one of these days, I'll be a little bit older and he'll be a little bit hungrier, and it'll be enough.

The weeks-old kiss still burns on my lips. I can still feel his hands on my body.

One day soon, maybe tonight, it will have to be enough.

The streets are quiet and it doesn't take long to get back to my apartment. We get out of his SUV without discussing it. Maybe he's just walking me to my door, but I don't think so. I think the dress worked.

His hand hovers in the small of my back as we climb the stairs.

My heart is pounding a mile a minute. I've wanted this for months now. Touched myself to a dozen different versions of how this might happen, and none of them felt like this. Not even kissing in New York felt like this, because that was a response. I'd goaded him into that.

This is different.

Terrifying. Exciting. Confusing.

Riddled with doubt.

In all my fantasies about my sister's bodyguard taking my virginity, I knew he wanted me. But the truth is, Scott's had zero problem keeping me at arm's length despite the chemistry between us.

So he thinks I'm pretty.

So he can't stop looking at my legs.

He's not a walking dick—part of why I'm attracted to him, I guess. But that control works against me, too.

If he says good night at the door, I'm going to need some serious ice cream therapy.

If he says good night at the door, I'm going to have to admit that I am a silly girl with a silly crush. And I don't want that to be true.

So when we get to my apartment, I slide the key into the lock, but I don't turn the handle. Not yet.

I want him to make the first move tonight.

A slow, rough exhale behind me kickstarts my heart. Then I feel his fingers on the nape of my neck. "You want me to come in?"

"I think you should either come in..." I say slowly, my pulse pounding so hard it hurts. "And if you don't...maybe you should stay gone."

"You think I can stay gone?"

"That's not my problem if you can't."

"Coming in is a bad idea."

"So is stringing each other along."

"That was never my intention."

"What was your intention?"

"You're young—"

"Not that young."

"Innocent."

"Not that innocent."

"Maybe I want you to be." His breath brushes against my ear as he presses his front to my back. "Because if you aren't innocent, then you're just as complicit in being a tease as I am."

My pulse pounds in my neck. "What?"

"You heard me." He slides one arm around my waist, banding me to him tightly. The other brushes my hair out of the way and he nips my neck. "Open the door, Ali."

This is happening.

I turn the handle and we shove inside. My backpack tumbles to the floor as Scott's arms tighten around me.

"I'm not teasing you," I whisper in the quiet. "I promise. We can do anything you want."

"Jesus," he rasps.

"Nobody needs to know, right?" I press back against him, wanting to feel him grind his erection against my bottom.

His breath slides hot and fast against my neck as he holds me tight. "That's right. This is our secret."

I spread my legs, rocking my ass back against his thighs. I wish I was taller. Maybe if I'd worn fuck-me boots, my legs would be long enough to get my cheeks at the right height to roll against his cock. But I can feel it, a heavy, hot brand in the small of my back, and just as telling, his hand presses firm against my belly.

I love the wrap of his arm around me. He's big, all of his muscles solid and bulging, but there's more to it than that—when Scott's holding me, I feel safe. Like he'd never let anything happen to me.

Nothing bad, anyway.

Would he ever let me fly? Let me be myself?

Let me be *his*?

"What do you want, Ali?" The rough, whispered nickname that only he uses makes me whimper. I want him to call me that when he's buried deep inside me. When he's lost control and taken me, hard and fast, and my name spills out of him because he just can't help it.

"I want to have sex with you."

He laughs in my ear. "Not going to happen."

"Who's the tease now?"

"We're not going to have sex."

"Then go away." I don't mean it, but what did he think I'd want?

"But I can make you come." The promise pulses through me like pure electricity. It burns so bright it hurts. "You want to come on my fingers, Ali?"

I nod.

"Turn around."

Legs shaking, I peel myself out from the curve of his warm, hard body and turn on the spot. He cups my face in his hands and crushes his mouth against mine, his kiss hungry and hard. He kisses me until we're both breathing hard and my lips are swollen, and then he licks his way out of my mouth, making me moan at the loss of his taste.

"Shh... I'm going to make you feel so good. Back against the wall. Hands...good girl. No touching me."

"Why not?" I want to touch him. I want to hold on to his arms and feel his biceps work as he pistons his fingers in and out of me. I want to run my fingertips over his mouth and feel his breath, hot and desperate, as he watches me come. And more than anything, I want to squeeze his cock and make him wish he didn't have this ridiculous boundary between us.

Okay, so I know why not.

He just laughs as he tugs my skirt up.

I shudder as his fingers graze my belly. He plays there for a minute, back and forth, working my skin into a maze of goosebumps. Then he tugs at the elastic waistband of my panties and slips his hand inside.

I gasp as he cups my entire sex in his hand. His fingers cover the space between my thighs, touching me everywhere, and I have a moment of feeling faint—hell, why do I want him to fuck me? His fingers alone feel too big to be inside me.

"You wet for me, Ali?"

"Yes," I breathe.

He squeezes me gently, then not so gently. Good, because I'm not a china doll.

Then he rocks his hand against me hard enough to push me against the wall. Even better. I shudder as he pulls away, but his next touch is the tip of his fingers right up my slit, and he growls as he discovers I wasn't lying about being wet.

I'm soaked for him and he slides right up to my clit, circling it quickly before delving deeper. Up and down he works me, teasing my entrance with his fingertips at first, then the barest insertion, up to his first knuckle, but always back to my clit.

His touch sends a riot of feelings through my body. Hot and cold prickles dance beneath my skin and my face flames bright, because nobody has done this to me before and that's both a crying shame—because it's oh my God so good—and amazing, too, because I'm pretty sure nobody else would know to walk the line between pleasure and pain for me.

Nobody else would know that while I may be a virgin, I don't want to be treated like a delicate flower.

I want—ahhhh—yes. One thick finger sliding inside me. I want the extra push at the end that makes me squeak, and then I want another finger added before I'm fully ready for it.

I want to be stroked with such confidence that I thump my head back against the wall to keep from falling forward against him.

I want everything Scott is doing to me, exactly the way he's doing it.

"Yes," I breathe. "Oh, God, yes. Just like that."

"Just like that?" He laughs a little as he scissors his fingers inside me. "You don't want me to go harder?"

I curse under my breath. "Yes, please."

"Tell me you want to come. Let me hear some dirty words drip off your beautiful lips."

"Please make me come." I pant as he thrusts into me again, harder this time. I press up onto my toes, but he keeps going, reaching deep inside me to find that spot that made me go all frantic. "I want to come on your hand," I add, my words getting twisted by a groan as he adds his thumb lazily into the mix, stroking back and forth over the top of my clit. "Ohmygod. No. Yes. Oh, yes."

"You're gorgeous," he mutters, pressing closer. His hand gets trapped between our bodies and I can feel his breath on my lips. "The most beautiful woman in the world. And one day soon, I'm going to fuck you into oblivion."

I cry out, the promise of him taking my virginity all that I need to fly apart. My entire body overheats and I shudder, over and over again, as he kisses and strokes and holds me through it.

Holy shit.

There are orgasms, and then there's getting finger-banged by Scott Mayfair in the dark of my living room. I let go of the wall and wrap my arms around his neck.

"I've got you," he says quietly as he lifts me into his arms and carries me toward my room.

"How do you know where my bed is?" I murmur into his shoulder.

He laughs. "One room place, Ali. Doesn't take a rocket scientist. Would you rather I'd stalked you?"

"Safest stalker ever."

He puts me down on the bed and climbs over me, tugging me against him.

We're cuddling.

I just came all over his hands and probably need to clean up or something, and his erection is hard and throbbing against my hip, and he's just...cuddling me.

"We should—"

"Nope," he says roughly. "You should go to sleep, study-girl."

"I want to make you come, too." I wiggle closer, reaching for him. "Don't you want to..."

But it doesn't take much for him to divert my wiggling fingers and tug my hands up to his chest. "Shhhh."

We go back and forth like that a few more times, my words getting more sluggish as his warmth gets under my skin and lulls me into dreamland.

[12]

SCOTT

THE NEXT MORNING Ali sends me a text first thing.

A: I had the best dream last night.

S: Tell me about it.

A: This hot guy I've been trying to hook up with for like, forever, came over...

S: Lucky guy

A: I was the lucky one

S: Tell me about it

A: Maybe you should come over again tonight

Maybe I should. I don't have a great reason to say no. But the next time we hook-up, it won't just be my fingers that feel her coming apart. Next time, I won't be able to keep my dick out of her, I'm afraid, and while I know she's fine with that...I'm still wrapping my head around it.

She's twenty.

An adult.

But just barely.

When I first went to war, she was in elementary school.
My phone chirps again.

A: Stop thinking so hard about it
S: Oh, I'm hard all right
A: That's better. Just a booty call. Don't worry, k?

But I am worried, in a way I've never been about a woman before. I need to blow something up to clear my mind. I swing by The Horus Group offices to see if anyone wants to hit a range with me. Cole and Jason are out, but their receptionist points me toward Wilson's office.

"It would be good to get him out, he's been locked in there for like thirty hours," she whispers.

"I have not," he calls out, and I'm still laughing when I prop myself against the door frame of his office.

I stop when I see what he's doing. On the six monitors in front of me are different camera angles inside a home. The occupants are home, and...busy. "Wow, man."

He glances over his shoulder. "Ah. Sorry. You can wait out there if you want."

"What the hell...who are you watching?" On the screen there were four people having sex. And one person was watching, curled up on a couch against the wall. There was something about her that was familiar. Long red hair, pale skin... "Is that...?"

He jams his finger against the keyboard and all the windows flip to his desktop. "Never mind."

"I don't want to know, do I?"

He shrugs. "We do crazy things for love, man."

"Speaking of crazy, I'm in the mood to shoot, you interested?"

"Sure."

We're all members of an indoor range below an office building on K Street. Officially, there aren't any indoor ranges in the District of Columbia. Unofficially, this one is close and convenient and very protective of its members' privacy.

Only the Secret Service has a better deal, and that's because their ammo is free.

Sometimes we get creative, but today I just want to unload my Browning High-Power a few hundred times. Wilson surprises me by pulling out a light Ruger SR22.

"Doing some plinking?" I ask as he shoots me the finger.

"It's a gift," he mutters.

"For the redhead?" It's still bugging me how familiar she looked.

"Forget you saw her."

"Deal." I don't need to worry about his woman problems. I've got my own. "You wrapped up in her?"

"Yeah. It's complicated."

"Isn't it always?"

He blinks at me. "Is it?"

"Has been for me."

"I wouldn't know. I've never...done this before."

I don't think he's talking about stalking a woman and sending her a gun. For Wilson Carter, that's probably a textbook definition of romance right there.

"I have. Fucked up my entire life. I'm pretty adamant about not doing it again."

"That why we're shooting today?"

I shrug. "Yeah. Maybe."

"Who is she?"

I could tell him.

"Nobody needs to know, right?"

"This is our secret."

No, I couldn't. "Someone I met at Georgetown."

"A student?"

"Yeah."

He gives me a look that says everything I've been thinking. I'm fifteen years past the point of dating co-eds. But one in particular has dragged me back into the land of flirting and teasing and hook-ups just for fun.

No drama, no worries.

"She's good for me," I finally say, loading my pistol. "Now let's see how many paper bad guys we can kill."

[13]

ALISON

Scott didn't come over last night.

That should be fine, because I promised him—and myself—that we were just having fun. No expectations.

But I'm still bummed.

So when my phone vibrates at my feet, ten minutes into my Research Methods class, I try to ignore it.

I try *hard*.

I last twenty seconds, tops, before I drop my pen and lean over to "pick it up," sneaking a glance at my phone in the process.

S: Sorry I went radio silent yesterday. Something came up. Heading to New York for a few days.

I stare at the screen, considering my options for responding. Really, there's only one thing to say.

A: No prob. Travel safe. Text when back.

My instructor's voice jerks me back to the class. "Ms. Reid, does whoever you're texting have something to share on this subject matter?"

I shove my phone in my bag, my cheeks flaming red as I straighten up. "I'm sorry, Professor. It won't happen again."

"See that it doesn't. And what assessment issues do you see in this particular example?"

I blink at the white board. *Shit*. In front of me, Corey clears his throat and taps on his notebook. In big, block letters, he's written **objectives=measurement=assessment**. A wave of relief rolls over me.

"They could correlate more closely to the objectives. It's not necessarily a fair measurement tool."

The instructor narrows her eyes at me, but then nods and moves on. I ignore my bag for the remainder of the class, and sag in relief when we're released.

"Thank you," I whisper, leaning over Corey's shoulder. "You just saved my butt."

"It's a butt worth saving," he teases, turning his head to look at me. I give him a reproachful look. "I know, and it's not a butt that's interested in me at all."

"And we don't talk about that, right?" It's too weird, how Corey brings that up from time to time. I lust after Scott incessantly, painfully, and I almost never bring it up with him.

Okay, maybe I'm being too hard on Corey.

So when he laughs and stands up, I stand up, too. We're friends.

And when he says, "You can make it up to me by coming to the casual mixer on Friday night," I say yes, because we're friends.

I'm not going to sleep with Corey, but I can hang out with him.

I sling my arm around his waist. "We'll find you a nice girl on Friday night. Okay?"

He shrugs. "Okay."

If only Scott were this easy to handle.

———

No more texts from Scott the rest of the week means that come Friday, I'm ready to party—as hard as senior level poli sci nerds go, which isn't that hard.

I get to McAllister Lounge shortly after eight, armed with bourbon and Coke and a jumbo bag of party mix. The social space on the top floor is unofficially reserved for upper years, and tonight someone has paid for a bouncer who is checking ID.

That's a problem.

I linger toward the back of the line, waiting for a glimpse of Corey. I might be the only senior who's not legal yet, and I don't want to put the bouncer in the awkward position of kicking me out if it can be avoided.

A girl three people ahead of me in line doesn't have her wallet. "Seriously?" she protests, hands on her hips. Tits out. Not a bad plan. "I walked over from my dorm." She waved her lanyard at him. "Anyone here can vouch for me. I take Modern International Relations with Saxon. Sax! Bud!"

It totally works. Saxon comes over and flashes his "my daddy's a senator" smile, and the girl is in. Anabeth? Anabelle? Whatever, she's in, it worked for her, I'm totally trying it. I shove my wallet deep into a skinny pocket inside my backpack, beneath the package of tampons I keep there, and hope that if Bouncer Guy decides to look inside my bag he doesn't want to dig past the lady supplies.

Before I get to the head of the line, Corey bounces into my side. "You made it!"

"Of course I did."

"You usually don't."

"But I owed you." I winked at him.

"You wound me. That's the only reason you're here, isn't it?"

Since I'm hoping Scott might be back tonight...yeah. "I promise, this is as exciting as my social life gets."

He snickers, slinging his arm around my shoulders. "You didn't get the party gene that your sister got?"

I stiffen and shrug off his arm. "Leave that alone."

"Shit. Sorry."

"It's okay. Just...not funny."

"Too soon?"

"Yep." We're at the head of the line and I give the bouncer my student card. He looks me up and down. "Driver's license?"

"Don't have one," I say with a warm, apologetic shrug. "But I promise I'm in my final year. I've got the study lines to prove it." I point at my eyes and squint.

He snorts and turns to Corey. "ID?"

Corey hands over his license and we're waved in. I add my drinks to the communal table and rip open the bag of party mix. Anabeth or Anabelle squeals about how much better pretzels are when they're mixed in with the other stuff—"'cause they get the powder on them! Ohmygod!"—and I'm reminded why I don't usually party hard.

Or at all.

I pour a big drink and find a seat in the middle of the room. Trick learned from being raised in a family of extroverts heavily involved in politics: it's easier to hide in plain sight and let the conversations swirl around you. If you hug the wall, someone well-meaning and totally clueless will try to drag you into a conversation you don't want to participate in. Or even worse—introduce you to someone they think will be your new bestie.

Always super awkward. Easier to dive right into the middle

and just go to the happy place in your head while people talk at you.

I pull out my phone, but Corey snatches it out of my hand. Where did he come from?

"Seriously? Are you doing some reading?"

"No." I snatch it back. "And don't touch my stuff."

"Don't be antisocial."

I glance at my messages. The exchange I got busted for in Research Methods is the last communication I've had with Scott. I take a deep breath and put the phone on silent. "Fine. I've turned it off for the night, are you happy?"

He grins. "I will be once we start dancing."

I roll my eyes. That is so not happening. I turn to Saxon. "Hey, do you have your summer research project lined up?"

Corey sighs. I ignore him. It's a casual mixer, not a rave. We can talk about course work. It's good practice for the rest of our lives.

[14]
SCOTT

S: Back in the city. Want to hang out later?

I FEEL like I've been gone back to my early twenties sending that message. That makes me shudder, because I was thinking with my dick then. Fuck, I'm thinking with my dick now. But... it's what Ali wants. And after abandoning her all week to go to New York and go six rounds with the Mayfair legal team and the British Consulate, I could use some chill time with a hot girl who likes me just for me. Maybe I haven't matured past my twenties after all.

She doesn't reply to my text right away. I move through my apartment, dropping my keys on the counter, my wallet beside them. I toe off my shoes then undo my tie.

She said she's only seen me in a suit.

When I pick her up tonight, I want her to see the real me, as much as I can share with her. The me that used to live in cargo pants and black t-shirts when I wasn't in fatigues.

I put on casual stuff and grab my phone again. No message back.

S: You studying? Want me to do a coffee run?

I fire up my laptop and check my email. Then I prowl into the kitchen. I don't have shit fuck all to make breakfast with. Maybe I should do a grocery run before inviting Ali back to my place. I grab my keys and wallet, throw on a hoodie, and head out the door.

Two bags of eggs, bread, milk, cheese and OJ later—plus vegetables and fruit, because I'm not actually a twenty-year-old goon—I'm back at my place, and still getting radio silence.

I pull out my phone to text her again, promising myself it's not needy if I'm concerned about her, when the screen lights up.

A: Sorry. So, so sorry. At a party.

I have zero right to get mad about that. She's an adult. A college student. And for the year that I've known her, totally responsible.

I'm still thinking "what fucking party" when she texts again.

A: Should be home by eleven. Midnight at the latest. Will text when I'm back.
S: I can pick you up.
A: It's cool. I'm with a friend. He'll walk me home.

And now I'm officially wondering who *he* is. The back of my neck heats up and I have to force myself to put the phone down before I crack it from gripping it too hard.

I count to fifty before replying.

S: You okay? Just say the word, and I can come get you.
A: Seriously, I'm good. It's a mixer.

I'm not sure I know what that means. In my world, it would mean cocktails with officers and NGO officials. And I wouldn't call it a party. I don't reply, because anything that would come out of my fingers would be inappropriate right now. I put away the groceries. When the phone chimes again, I take my time reaching for it.

A: What are you wearing?

That mollifies me a bit. She might be with a guy, but she's thinking about me. And maybe the guy is a total dork.

S: Not a suit
A: Tease! Pics or it didn't happen
S: I'm not taking a selfie
A: I will if you will

And just like that, I'm trying to take a picture of myself without looking like a menace. I settle for a body shot, no face. It only took six rejected pictures to get one that was acceptable. Ten seconds later she fires back a picture of herself reclining on a couch, full glass of something dark in her hand. She's wearing a long-sleeve black shirt and jeans, her hair is down, and she looks so good my dick aches.

S: I think it's midnight
A: hahaha

I'm not joking. I want her, and I want her now.

S: Are you on campus? I'm coming to pick you up.
A: Fine. But I'll meet you downstairs. And don't rush. I've
just stumbled into a conversation I can actually stand.

She texts the address, and I do as she instructs. I go to Starbucks, get us coffee—boring old man drip for me, a vanilla latte for her—and head to campus, taking my time. When I get there, I find a parking spot not far from the building she's in and wait.

And wait.

Thirty-five minutes later, I text her.

No answer.

I've got two choices. I can keep waiting, or I can go up and see if she needs rescuing.

I can already hear her protesting that I've shown up, but I can play Hailey's bodyguard or something. I know how to be subtle.

Heading inside, I scan the main floor for her, just in case she's waiting inside. Nothing, so I take the elevator upstairs. The only lights on in the building were a single office on the third floor, unlikely to be the site of a student party, and a bunch of windows were lit up on the top floor. Probably a lounge of some sort.

As soon as the elevator doors open, I hear an argument.

"Time for you to head home," an authoritative voice insists.

"We hired you to keep other people out, not tell us we're having too much fun." A female voice, but not Ali.

I turn the corner and see two young people being blocked from re-entering the open space beyond by a large black man who looks like he's not going to be swayed. Poor guy.

I give him an easy smile, security-guy-to-security-guy. "Hey, man. I'm here to pick someone up. Alison Reid."

He consults his clipboard and nods. "She's here."

"Can I...?" I point past him.

He shakes his head. "Private party."

I pull out my wallet and hand over a card. He takes one look at The Horus Group logo and waves me past.

I wait until the drunk kids can't see my face to snicker at their protests fading behind me. But my gloating doesn't last long, because on the far side of the lounge, on a couch facing away from the entrance, Ali's wrapped up in the arms of a kid. A guy, she'd say, but I just see a hundred and thirty pounds of privilege and a drooling dick. He's trying to kiss her and she's pushing against his chest, laughing uneasily.

I see it all through a red haze.

"What the fuck?" I bark out, reaching over the couch and shoving the kid to the floor. Ali scrambles to her feet, clearly pissed.

"Scott!"

"Behind me, Ali."

"Stop it, he's drunk. It's fine."

I move around the furniture, getting between them. I shoot her a quick glance over my shoulder. "Did you want him to touch you?"

"No, but—"

I pick the loser up off the floor like he's made of paper and shove him, hard, against the wall. His head snaps back and thunks against the brick. That's gonna hurt tomorrow.

So will the Hulk-fist-sized bruise I'm about to give him on his cheek. I pull my arm back and Ali latches on to it. "Stop!" She twists so she's between us. "Don't do something you'll regret."

"I guaran-fucking-tee you I won't regret smashing this asshole's face in."

"I was handling it."

"I was waiting downstairs for a half hour. How long has he been crawling on you?"

She winces. "Sorry."

"You have nothing to be sorry for. Out of my way."

Behind her, the kid groans and crumbles to the ground. I roll my eyes, and Ali presses her hands against my chest. "Let's go. I'm fine."

I shrug her off and crouch down, fisting the front of his shirt hard enough he whimpers. He's an emo little shit, nothing but skin and bones, and he's fucking petrified. Good. "Leave her alone. She's not interested in your tiny little dick, or your pathetic feelings, or anything else, got it?"

His eyes go wide and start to fill with tears. Jesus.

I sneer and drop him back to the floor.

Ali sighs, the sound magnified in the sudden silence. The entire party has stopped and is watching us. I stand up, and stare down at him for a beat before I turn to look at her.

She's pissed at *me*. Her eyes are wide and her mouth is small, her lips pressed tight together. Without a word, she yanks her backpack off the ground, spins around and heads for the exit. She doesn't wait for the elevator, taking the stairs instead, and she flies down each flight. I'm right behind her, but I don't catch up to her until we're on the ground floor.

"Wait. Alison! Wait!" I hook my fingers around her upper arm and spin her around.

She shoves me hard in the chest, but I don't move. I let go of her, though. I'm not an idiot. She paces backward, shaking her head at me. "What the hell was that?"

She bumps back against the door and shoves it open, and we spill out into the night. It's cold enough that she pulls up short and rummages in her bag, pulling out a jacket. Her movements are short and jerky as she shoves her arms into the sleeves and yanks it tight around her body.

"That was..." I exhale roughly. "That was me reacting to a guy mauling you."

"There's protecting me and then there's using me as an excuse to flood the room with testosterone. That was way over the line."

"I didn't even hit him. Anything less would have been unacceptable." It grates on me that she doesn't see herself as precious enough to be worth such protection.

"He's my friend! And he's drunk. Now you've terrified him."

"He was all over you!"

"I was fine!"

"No you weren't!"

She opens her mouth, then snaps it shut into a tight, unyielding line. I don't know if she finally sees it the way I do or if she just doesn't want to keep yelling at each other in the middle of campus. I sigh and point in the direction of my SUV. "Let me take you home."

She nods, but it's tight, and she's not quite looking at me.

Shit.

The ride is short and silent. When I pull up in front of her place, she doesn't get out right away. She exhales slowly, then looks down at her hands. "Thank you, I guess."

My eyebrows hit the roof. I wasn't expecting that. I don't know how I feel about it, honestly. "I don't want you to say thank you. Especially not if you don't mean it."

She looks out the window. "I hear what you're saying. How it looked. You could have gotten mad at me and you didn't."

What the fuck? "I wouldn't have. Even if it wasn't obvious

that he was all over you and you didn't want it...I know you, Ali. That's not you."

"He asked me to go to the party with him."

"So? Did he ask you to make out on the couch with him?"

She doesn't say anything. Fuck.

"Let me make something crystal clear, babe. No guy worth his balls expects something like that. And the guys that do, deserve to have their balls cut off with a rusty fucking machete. My reaction back there was big, but it was also tempered. I wanted to rip him limb from limb. Got it?"

"Yeah."

"Come on. Let me walk you up."

I get out and jog around the truck, opening her door for her.

She stares straight ahead as we cross the street. But when we get to the wide steps at the front of her building, she doesn't punch in her code. I do an automatic scan of the surroundings. We're alone. It's late, and relatively private, and if she doesn't want me to walk her upstairs, I'm not going to push it.

I lean against the wall. If she wants to talk, I'll talk, but I'm not going to open my giant ape mouth without prompting. I've done enough tonight.

She scuffs her toe against the stoop. "Was that just you being protective tonight?"

Wow. She's heading straight into the middle of the land mines. "I don't know how to answer that. I don't like seeing another guy touch you."

"You don't touch me."

"I did. I will again."

She lifts her chin a bit, but she's still not looking at me.

"You mess with my head in a way that's distressing for a grown man, Ali."

That gets her attention. She jerks her face up and blinks at me. "What?"

"You gotta know I'm twisted up over you."

She blanches. Well, that was the wrong thing to say. Fuck me.

"I was jealous. When I saw him touching you. Okay? That was my first reaction, for a split-second. Then I was just being protective. I swear."

"I don't want you to be...I don't want you to expect feelings from me," she says quietly.

What the hell? "I already told you I don't expect anything. But feelings are just human nature. Don't read too much into it because I don't want some pipsqueak touching what I feel is all mine right now."

"All yours?"

"I warned you I don't share."

"I know." She licks her lips. "I don't want anyone else."

"I know."

"I'm just being me, you know. Now. I was...trying too hard before. But now...this is me."

"That makes it even worse."

"Oh, great, thanks."

"That's not what I mean." I laugh gently. "You're hot. Just the way you are. Distractingly so."

She scowls at me. "It's hard not to feel like I'm being blamed for having tits."

I laugh again, because she doesn't give an inch. Nor should she. But that doesn't change the fact that I'm defenseless around her, and I'm not dealing with that well. "I'm not blaming you. I promise. That would make me just as bad as that douche at the party."

She shakes her head, a small smile playing on her lips. "Not at all. And his name is Corey, by the way."

"I don't care what his name is." She smirks and I pull her in for a hug. "I should go."

She nods against my chest. "Just for tonight. We could use a breather."

"You're being way more mature than me about this."

She winks. "Don't worry. I'll go back to being a selfie-loving co-ed any second now."

"Can I kiss you goodnight?"

"You better."

I crowd her against the brick wall, taking my time to touch my lips against hers. Savoring this moment, the only one I'll get tonight. I'm going to make it good for both of us, good enough it makes up for my Neanderthal show earlier.

Her nose brushes mine as she stretches up. I cup her cheek. Her skin is so soft, but beneath it she's made of steel, honed by two decades of bracing against the Dashford Reid hostility. And now I'm yet another problem for her to manage.

"I really am sorry about tonight," I mutter, my lips bumping against hers.

"Shut up. Kiss me. Feel bad later."

I can do all three.

Her lips part immediately as I slide our mouths together, her teeth nipping at my bottom lip as I suck her top one into my mouth. I groan and haul her tighter against me, thrusting my tongue into her mouth. Fuck. She tastes sweet, coke and bourbon and pure Ali beneath it all, wet and hot and eager for me to fill her up. Her tongue swipes at mine. She wants to play, and the thought sends a dangerous spark through my body.

How dirty can this kiss get outside her building?

I hitch her up my body, cupping her ass as I shift one of my thighs between hers. She rubs against me, squeezing her legs as I work my hand inside her jacket.

The whole time, I'm exploring her mouth, finding out what strokes make her wriggle, what licks make her moan.

My fingers find her waist, her ribs, and I follow the path up to her breast. Through the thin fabric of her shirt I can feel lace and structured fabric. She's wearing a fancy bra.

My cock throbs at the second-base promise of silk and satin.

But not tonight. I keep sliding my hand, up over her nipple, ignoring her breathless protest as I cup the nape of her neck. I deepen the kiss one last time and pull away, ignoring how wet and shiny her mouth is—if I think about that for even a second, I'll be a goner. "Good night, Ms. Reid."

She presses her fingers to her lips, a smile playing behind the long, slim digits. "Good night, Mr. Mayfair," she whispers, her eyes dancing.

We stand there, frozen, until she giggles and I step back. She turns and lets herself in, and I let myself ogle her sweet ass peaking out beneath her jacket until she's inside the apartment building and the door closes in my face.

My phone vibrates as I walk away from her building. I turn around once I'm across the street and look up. Her apartment is dark, then the window brightens a bit as she opens the door. I look down at my phone. The text message is from her.

A: 1/2

That's it. But then another bubble appears, and I realize she's sent me a photo text, it's just taking its sweet-ass time to load.

It's a selfie, taken in the stairwell. She's giving the camera a little smile that doesn't reach her eyes. Does she regret sending me away? She was right to, of course. But damn it if I don't want to be upstairs with her right now.

1/2...One of two...

I stand there and wait for the second photo. My attention is divided between my phone, still working away with the download, and the two windows of her apartment—she walked through the dark living space and now she's in her small bedroom. I can picture the room. Her closet, already over-flowing with clothes. That little double bed, pushed into the corner, with the faded quilt and basic cotton sheets.

The standing mirror, where I can picture her looking at herself as she gets dressed.

As she gets undressed.

As she touches herself, maybe, because she's a girl that sends me pictures, so maybe she's a girl who watches herself get off.

I'm jealous of that mirror, for getting a daily glimpse at her soft, lithe body.

It's been offered to you, jackass. Over and over again, and I keep turning her down. And then tonight, if I hadn't pushed my luck and shown my hand, shown how desperate I am for her, I could have had another offer.

One of these days, she's going to offer, and I'm going to take every inch she gives me and then some.

Then the second picture comes in.

A: 2/2

And it's hot as fuck. Skin, everywhere. Nothing exposed, nothing that would end up in the tabloids—she's learned that lesson well. One arm over her breasts, one leg twisted up to cover what I already know is the sweetest pussy in the entire fucking world.

Her tongue, caught between her teeth.

But it's the look on her face that does me in. Naked, unvar-nished need, and I'm swearing under my breath, because my heart is already across the street and punching in her security code, and that can't happen.

One of these days just might have been tonight, if I wasn't stupid.

S: I deserve to go home and have a cold shower. You're fucking gorgeous. I'll be less of an ass tomorrow.
A: Then maybe we can hang out tomorrow nite
S: I'm going to hold you to that
A: Hold me however you want...once you're out of the doghouse

Fuck. I shake my head and laugh as I head back to my vehicle.

ALISON

I WAIT until the next day to message Corey. I'm tempted not to at all, but we've got another month of class together, and I don't want it to be more awkward than it needs to be.

He doesn't reply.

That's fine.

I get some reading in over breakfast, then Hailey texts and asks me if I want to go to yoga with her and Tegan. I pass, but it reminds me that the most cardio I've done in a week is grinding against Scott's leg last night, and I throw on my running shoes. I kept off the freshman fifteen by diligently logging the miles, but in the last year and a half, my running has fallen down the priority list.

Those ramen noodles won't work themselves off.

When I get home, I throw myself into the shower, which makes me think of Scott last night. He'd said he'd go home and take a cold shower.

I hope he didn't. I hope he got himself off instead. My skin flushes, nothing to do with the hot water beating down on me, as I picture him naked. Hard. Holding himself.

My hand slips between my legs, over my trimmed curls, and

into the slippery wetness that spontaneously happens whenever I think of him.

All those muscles straining...would he lean forward, brace himself against the wall as his hand moved faster? I rub my clit and close my eyes, picturing him jerking off on his bed instead. Laying on his back, watching me through almost-closed eyes as I perch between his legs and tell him to make himself come. Tell him I want to taste it once he does.

My cheeks burn at the idea.

Maybe tonight I'll invite him over so I can give him a blow job.

Then I'll crawl into his lap and ride his hand again. I try to slide two fingers into myself, but it's not the same. His touch lights me up in a way I can't replicate, so I don't try. I find my clit again and roll two fingers over it now, imagining they're the thick pad of his thumb. That he's right beneath me, teasing me with his cock.

I want him inside me like I've wanted nothing else in my entire life. I start to clench for him, clench at nothing, and the ache of that sends me spinning into a bright, hungry climax that makes me shudder and quake, but still leaves me wanting more.

I slump to the floor of the shower and tip my face into the water.

Good Lord. I hope he's not busy tonight.

He's going to get a hell of a text once I've finished my International Relations study notes.

[16]
SCOTT

9:05 PM.

That's what the time on my phone reads when Ali texts me. The time when I realize, this is actually happening. We've danced around it for ages, but now we see each other, truly, and we still dig each other.

A: I've been studying all day.
S: Good girl.
A: I have been. Worked really hard. And now...

My heart thuds in my chest. My cock thickens, straining at my fly.

S: Now?
A: Wanna come over?

I'm at her door twenty minutes later. She answers in a black tank top and grey sweatpants, and I've never seen anything sexier.

"Hey," she says, and that's as much conversation as is going to happen before I'm balls deep in her.

Maybe.

Fuck, I'm nervous. I've run into gunfights with more confidence than I have as I peel off her shirt, baring a black satin bra that's simple and fancy as fuck at the same time.

I'm not sure if I can take her virginity, but I can sure as hell make her come again. Christ, I've missed the feel of her clenching hard around my fingers. I want to taste that flood as she rides my face.

"Bed," she gasps as I lift her up, palming her ass through soft cotton that has to go, now. I kiss her neck, sucking on the flesh there, then lower, tasting her collarbone and her shoulder. I use my teeth to pull down her bra strap, and she grabs at the other one, baring both of her breasts.

I almost drop her as her tits bounce into view.

She's perfect. They're perfect. Round and firm, topped with nipples that are already tightening under my gaze. I set her down and drop to my knees. I nuzzle the skin between her breasts, then take my time kissing both mounds before I suck one tight peak into my mouth.

I almost jizz in my pants at the sweet fullness in my mouth, the rub of her taut nipple against my tongue. So fucking good. Sexy and lush, I can't wait to have these beauties slapping me in the face as she bounces on top of me. I ease off her pants, then stand, replacing my mouth with my hands. No way am I leaving her breasts unattended. I'll be their faithful servant for the rest of the night.

For fucking ever if she wants.

Ali palms my dick through my pants and I hoarsely tell her to get me naked. She starts with my shirt, unbuttoning it. Her fingers are shaking, and I stop her long enough to pull her hand to my mouth and kiss the tips. "We'll go slow," I promise.

She laughs. "Slow is the last thing I want. I'm so excited I can't handle it."

Well, all right then.

Eyes on her the whole time, I wrench down her panties and lift her up, my palms big and rough on her hips. Fuck, she's tiny. And she's breathing fast, because some brute is manhandling her onto her bed.

But when she lands on her back, she doesn't scurry away from me. Slow as honey, she rolls her knees up between us, her ankles crossing—obscuring my view of her pussy.

My pussy. For tonight, it's mine.

I'm going to lick it.

Suck it.

Finger it until she screams.

Claim it in every way I can without ruining her forever.

I get rid of my clothes and crawl on top of her, our mouths finding each other, her hands wrapping around my back as I tangle my fingers in her hair.

Her legs wrap around my waist, and I forget about all my virtuous plans to make her come on my fingers and with my tongue, because she's already wet, and I can feel her pussy against my balls.

She freezes.

I kiss her harder, not ready to talk about going to the next step—or not.

She comes alive in my arms again and rolls her hips, and my cock slips between her lips, lying against her sex.

I match her movements, heat swarming my entire body as I rut against her.

"Scott," she breathes, and I brush my thumb across her cheekbone.

"Ali."

"You feel...wow."

I grin at her, then I glance down between our bodies.

It's obscene, this view of my cock sliding between her legs.

Beautiful, how wet she is for me. How slick her slit is, making me glide faster, rub harder.

That's us. Beauty and the beast. My arms flex as I hold myself above her, surging our bodies together.

Almost fucking.

It's even more perverted like this.

"See how much I'd fill you up," I rasp, and she jerks her head up.

She was already watching, but now she's looking right at me again. Like she sees every twisted want in my head and they get her off. Blood pounds through my body. She licks her lips and the throb in my cock hurts so bad now.

"Yeah, I see," she whispers. "You're so big. You'll never fit."

That shouldn't turn me on. It never has before, not like this. Not this fantasy. But it totally does. She writhes beneath me, taunting me to play, too. Fuck, yes. I press her legs wide and grind against her, my cock riding hard over her clit and onto her belly again. "I'd break you, Ali."

"I want you to." She reaches for me, winding her arms around my neck, and she tugs me down.

I could hold myself up. I could resist her. Make us both watch as her breath grows shallow, as her nipples tighten and her tits flush.

But if I let her bring me close for a kiss, if she wraps her legs around my hips, it's going to feel...

"Oh," she gasps, as the angle between us shifts, and suddenly, my cock is right there.

She's so wet. It's such a mindfuck, knowing I could just slam into her. Knowing just as clearly that I can't.

I can't.

My dick didn't get the message. He's drooling hard, a big fucking puppy dog barking at the park.

I don't have a condom on. She's never done this before.

We can't.

She rolls her hips, and the tip—*just the tip*, holy fuck, it's a wet dream come true—notches into place.

Yes. My mind scrambles with how good this feels.

"We can't," I mutter, and it's so guttural I'm not even sure it's English.

She kisses me, hot and frantic, her breath puffing against my mouth as she licks at me and looks down between us and then kisses me again.

"Come on," she says. "Just a little bit. I just wanna feel you..." She whimpers as I press my hips. Just a little bit.

What she wants.

He's not going in any further, not without one of us working hard for it. My balls pull tight, begging to blow their load in a virgin pussy, and she wants it. I want it. I can't remember why this is a bad idea.

Two consenting adults.

A fucking shared craving that isn't going anywhere, no matter what we do.

Heat and need are swirling around me now, binding me to her, but I can't do this. I pull back, and this time I don't let her hold me close. She growls beneath me, fierce and proud, and I haul her up and off the bed, holding her against me as I spin us so I'm sitting against her headboard and she's on my lap.

My cock is safely wedged between us, his wet tip angrily slapping my belly.

"You want me inside you, Ali?"

She winds her hands into my hair. "You know I do. You still got a virgin hang-up or something?"

I laugh, harsh and hollow. Or something. "You being a virgin isn't a problem."

She smirks. "I know it turns you on." She licks her lips. "It turns me on, too. I wasn't kidding when I said I want you to break me."

"I'm not doing that to you. That's not what sex is, Ali."

"You going to teach me? I want to know every last dirty thing you know."

"That's why God invented Tumblr. You don't need me to teach you." My dick disagrees, and Ali makes this hungry little sound in her throat as my erection throbs between her legs.

She rocks down my length. Back up again. Then she stops and grabs my hands. She presses them to her hips, then slides them up to her breasts. I love her tits so much. They're ripe and firm and surprisingly heavy.

They're fucking womanly. She's making a point. Has *been* making it, and I've been missing it, and it's a miracle she hasn't punched me for being stupid.

We're both breathing hard, and she whispers my name. I jerk my attention from her nipples—can't blame me, come on, they're perfect—to her face.

"I'm not a kid," she says softly. "I haven't done this with anyone else because I'm kind of fucked up about sex and I don't want to be. I don't want to be ashamed, either, though, and I won't let you turn me into some virginal innocent girl. Not unless it's a game. Okay?"

None of this is okay, not really. But Ali? Fuck, there's nothing wrong with her. I nod and move my hands of my own volition this time, cupping her face. "You aren't fucked up about sex. And there's nothing to be ashamed about between us."

"Then why aren't you inside me?" Her voice is soft and sweet, but strong.

She deserves the truth. "Because I'm the fucked up one. I'm

having trouble separating fantasy from reality here, and trying to be a good guy."

A smirk tells me my goal is way off the mark. "Get a condom on, mister. I want to have sex, and I want to have sex with you. I want you to call me a good girl and use all the dirty words, and when we're done, I'm probably going to want to do it again."

How the fuck can I say no to that?

I tumble her onto her back and reach for my pants on the floor. I roll the condom on as I crawl between her legs, but I don't thrust into her yet. I enter her with my fingers first, watching her face as she takes one, then two. That's fucking tight, but she's bucking hard against me.

"Another one," she breathes. "Stretch me wide. Get me ready."

Ali's no innocent. Gotta love the internet. I slowly add a third finger, and it's too tight, but she presses against me until she can't go any further, then I ease back. Before she can frown at me, I slide in again, getting past the knuckles this time.

When I pull out again, I wrap my hand around my cock, smearing her wetness on the condom.

She's as ready as she's going to get.

[17]

ALISON

My heart is pounding a mile a minute as I watch Scott press his erection against my pussy. I rock my hips, wanting him inside me with a restless impatience I can't even handle, but then he shifts, and he's *inside me*, just a little bit, and it's ohmygod so much bigger than his fingers.

I cry out and he pauses. He doesn't pull back, and he gets a gold star in de-virgining for that. He just looks at me and tells me how hot I am.

That helps.

I roll my hips, then plant my feet on the bed, but that tenses everything up.

"Shhh," he says, shifting so more of his weight is on top of me. Oh, I like that.

He kisses me, his tongue coaxing mine out to play, and then, ever so slowly, he pushes inside me, pausing every time I tense to whisper something else. Bit by bit I open to him, and he presses his hips forward until he's filling me up.

I'm gasping for air by the time he's buried to the root inside me, because I've never in my entire life felt anything like this.

I'm so full it hurts, but the hurt is so good, and I want him to do something, but I'm not sure what. Fuck me, probably.

I breathe his name, and he presses his hips into me. How is that possible, to get any deeper? But it is, and he does, and then he starts to pull out.

Before I can say something—*no no no*, maybe, or *get back here, asshole*, or *don't move, please*—he thrusts all the way into me, making me scream. And then I know exactly what I want to say.

"Again. Oh my God, do that again."

He grins, and does exactly that, dragging his cock out of me and driving it back in, tripping a bunch of really awesome nerve endings in both directions. I cling to him as he rocks into me, and when I start rolling my hips enthusiastically, he shifts positions, pushing up onto his knees.

He hauls me up with him, so my hips are off the bed and in his lap. I can't move as he holds my thighs steady, and he feeds his cock back into me. This angle is even better, because I'm all relaxed and open to him, and deep inside, the thick, broad head of his erection is rubbing something that feels so, so good.

I'm going to explode.

I mean, I'm going to come, but in a new and scary way, and I think it's a legit concern that I might actually burst into a million pieces.

People don't actually die from sex, right? Not unless there are gerbils involved?

I'm probably safe. I hope I don't actually explode. As soon as all those pieces of me slam back together, I'm going to want to do this again.

My hands roam onto my body. I want to touch him, too, but I can only reach his knee. But there's another part of him I can touch. The part that's ruthlessly spearing into me, over and over again. I slide my fingers over my mound. Holy shit, I'm wet.

Well, that would be embarrassing if he wasn't so hard. And huge.

All of that is inside me, I think as my fingers dance over his surging flesh. My touch centers all of my attention right there, where we're joined. It feels good, but underneath the "holy shit full of feelings" reaction, there's a burn, too. I'm going to be sore later.

That's later's problem.

"Touch yourself," Scott rasps, and I jerk my gaze to his face. He's watching, too.

"I'm touching you."

"And I'm going to fill you up with come in a minute, so either touch that pretty little clit and make yourself come, or get that gorgeous hand out of the way so I can do it."

Well. I grin and touch myself. "Like that?"

He groans. "Fuck yeah."

"You like watching?"

He groans. Okay, he's not one for talking right in the middle of sex.

I think I might be, though. We'll have to test that out. "I got myself off in the shower, thinking about watching you jerk yourself off."

Another groan, and his steady pace falters.

"I wanted to lick it up after—" I shriek as he shoves me...up the bed, sort of. I don't know, exactly. One minute I was touching myself and he was above me, then he was on top of me and my hand is trapped between our bodies. His mouth is next to mine, sharing harsh, desperate breaths as he slams into me, harder and faster until I seize up around him.

With a few harsh jerks, he comes with me.

As my heart rate returns to normal, I realize I've bit him on the shoulder.

His hands are fused to my ass. He grabbed me so hard I might have bruises in the morning.

I can feel his heart thudding against mine.

Wow.

"So..." I say breathlessly. "Sex is kind of fun."

[18]
SCOTT

ALI IS INSATIABLE. Even though it's her last month of classes and she's got final papers and exams to study for, she's texting me almost every night.

I'm not complaining. The sex is fantastic.

But that's all we're doing. At first her school work and my occasional trip back and forth to New York are good covers, but eventually I realize that...sex is really, genuinely all she wants.

I'm a fucking pussy, because I'm a little hurt by that. Which isn't fair to a woman like Ali, who has managed to have a healthy sexual relationship right out of the gate, no strings attached. She could teach me a thing or two if I wasn't such a stubborn idiot.

Instead, I decide to push the question and fuck up what is a perfect booty call relationship.

It's been two days since I've been over there, so I'm guessing tonight she's going to want a late night visit. I send a pre-emptive shot across the bow.

S: Studying late tonight? Want a dinner break?

A: I'll get a sandwich at the cafeteria. But I'll let you know when I'm done...

I let it go, and pick her up at the library at half-past ten, right on schedule. We go back to her place and she offers me ice cream, which leads to lick it off each other's torsos and slow, amazing sex on a chair in the middle of her kitchen. She rides me and I lick the last bit of sweet cream off her tits.

It's not until we've cleaned up and she's packing me out the door that I remember that I'm irrationally grumpy about this.

I lean against the door frame and pull her close for a lingering goodbye kiss. And then I push her again. "Let's go out for dinner tomorrow night. Italian. I know this place in Arlington..."

She shifts uncomfortably. "We don't need to go out for dinner."

"But I want to. With you."

"I've got a lot of studying to do."

"After your exams, then. No rush."

"I'll be diving right into my senior project."

"Alison."

She rolls her eye and mimics my serious voice. "Scott."

"Fine." I stand up straighter and cross my arms.

She raises her eyebrows. When I don't say anything else immediately, she sighs and takes off her shirt.

"You have gotten exceptionally comfortable with this sex thing," I say. "Not complaining."

She runs her fingers along the edge of her bra. This one is red with a few extra straps that make me think of tying her down. And I'm complaining about her being a dirty girl?

"It's not a big deal," she says, her chin jutting in a way that says, *right?*

"It was a big deal to me," I admit.

"That's because you're a dirty old man. It's an artificial construct, really."

"Maybe." I lick my lips. I'm getting hard. "It gets you off, too."

"Only because it was with you, and you are hot. It's the billionaire and the virgin role-play fun." Direct hit, and she knows it. She drops her hands to her yoga pants and tucks her thumbs in, playing up the ingénue. I don't need to hide that I'm turned on, so I lower my hand and squeeze my cock. She turns pink.

So much for me leaving in a huff. I roll my lower lip between my teeth and wait to see where she takes it.

"Are you still mad at me...sir?"

"No, I'm not not mad."

"Have I done something wrong?"

I want to take her over my lap and spank her something fierce, but the only one who's done something wrong tonight is me. "Come here, little one." She comes closer and I take her hand and press it against my erection. "Does that feel like I'm mad?"

"No, sir."

"Then drop to your knees and be thankful I'm so kind."

Her eyes light up. Jesus.

In a flash, she's got my cock out and her lips are wrapped around the head. "Like this?" she asks, pulling off with a pop.

I smirk. "You can take me deeper than that."

"I'll try," she says, sliding a nervous tremble into her voice. My dick throbs in response and she stifles a grin.

"Brat. Suck me off, or I'll come on your face."

She scowls and licks me like a lollipop.

And so it goes. I might be annoyed, but I'm not so principled that I won't take whatever she's offering. Especially when what she's offering is the best thing I've ever had.

I KNOW what I'm doing when I text Scott at four in the morning a few days later.

He knows what I'm doing, too.

That's why he shows up twenty-three minutes later, freshly showered with a condom in his pocket and a barely dissolved breath mint on his tongue.

I smirk as he looms over me. "You are such a dirty old man."

"We need to stop doing this."

He doesn't mean it, but I let him have this conversation. He's slowly wearing me down. I cross my arms and smile at him. "Why?"

"Because you're twenty and I'm not. Because I want to take you on a fucking date and you won't. Because we wind up yelling at each other half the time."

"But the rest of the time you're inside me and it feels so good, right?"

His eyes darken and I don't need to look down to know he's hard for me.

I love that.

I'm taunting him, working him into a lather in the hopes

that he'll fuck me so hard I won't be able to walk straight tomorrow.

"Yeah it feels good, you crazy woman. Why can't you sleep?"

"I just finished a practice exam—aced it—and was feeling restless, I guess. Full of *ohmygodimaybeknowit* energy."

"Full of what?"

"Oh my God I maybe know it."

He shakes his head and tugs me closer. "I'm sure you know it backwards and inside out. Come on, let's get naked. A few orgasms are exactly the sleep prescription you need."

"You were totally just thinking something about kids these days, weren't you?"

"I'll never tell."

Instead of leading him into my room, I take off my clothes and go and start the shower.

He follows, watching me silently. We've done it on my couch and on a chair in my kitchen, but we haven't had shower sex yet.

Since I owe him an apology, this feels like a good symbol. Washing away the bad juju or something. I start the shower and step into my small tub, holding the curtain out of the way. "Come here."

He follows, naked now as well. An amused smile curls up his lips. "It's the middle of the night."

"And I've been sweating bullets over international law for like eighteen hours. I don't smell good."

"You always smell fantastic," he mutters, but he joins me, crowding me into the water. I love how big he is, and how he uses that size to make me feel dominated in all the right ways. I turn to offer him some body wash, but the bottle tumbles out of my hand as he lifts me up. From nowhere he makes a condom appear, and I rip it open.

"Put it on me." The man thinks I'm way more gymnastic than I really am, but I reach between us and sheath him.

Then he's inside me in one, breath-stealing surge.

"Don't care if you've been working all day and night," he mutters, grinding against my clit as I pulse around him, adjusting to his size. "Want you anyway. Always."

I tighten my arms around his neck. So much for me making this about him. I close my eyes as he kisses my neck. Tighten my legs around his waist as he fucks up and into me. Basically hold on as he ravages me, because this is hard and fast and rough.

"You've got me. Always," I promise. I'm a shitty girlfriend, because I'm focused on a dozen life goals that have nothing to do with a man, but Scott likes that about me. "I'm yours, you know that?"

"At four in the morning," he growls.

"And when I'm buried in a pile of books, or taking an exam..."

"Am I?"

"Yes."

"Am I?"

I cry it out this time. "Yes!"

"Fuck." He growls as he splits me in two, his hands tight on my thighs and his cock a piston between my legs. I don't even need to touch myself, because he's hitting all the right spots: his cock is stretching my cunt, bumping my cervix and a bunch of other good spots inside; the root of him rolls my clit with each buried thrust; but most effective of all are his words, squeezing my heart in my chest.

Hell, I didn't even know that thing worked.

"Always yours," I whisper, my voice having fled the building. My words crack a little as I try to ride him, desperate to come with him.

His hands slide, big and sure, to my ass, squeezing my

cheeks and pulling them apart. Pulling *me* apart as he holds me steady and fills me, over and over again, until I'm sobbing his name and climbing the peak he always manages to get me up and over.

"Ali," he growls. "My Ali. Mine. Fucking mine, always."

"Yes," I say, but it's not really a word, it's a cry, and it's lost in the water as I tip my head back and explode for him. He buries himself in me, his cock twitching as it spills his seed inside that condom.

I wish he was bare inside me.

We should talk about that. I'm ready. I trust him.

But baby steps. I laugh shakily as he sets me down and gets rid of the condom.

"Is that a sleep deprivation laugh?" he asks roughly as he wraps his arms around me from behind.

I shake my head. I don't need any secrets from him. "I was just thinking maybe we should talk about going without condoms."

He doesn't move, but his heart is pounding. I can hear it. "Yeah?"

"I'm...I get the shot. And if you..."

"I'll get tested. It's been a while, but another test is a good thing."

I nod. "And I was laughing because I was thinking it's a weird order."

"What is?"

I turn in his arms. "That I don't have any problem suggesting we go bare, but I've been struggling with agreeing to..."

He smirks at me. "To...?"

"Tomorrow night is my last exam." I press up on my toes and kiss his jaw, then lick down his strong, corded neck. "If you want to go out and celebrate with me..."

His Adam's apple jumps against my lips. "Yeah?"

I grin. That was worth it. "Yeah."

"You don't have friends you'd rather go out with?"

I laugh. "You scared off my only friend."

"I didn't scare him off, I just asserted my claim."

"And yet I'm not going out for drinks with anyone."

"So I'm the last option for filling your social calendar." He groans, so I bite the tendon between his neck and his shoulder. "Hey! Brat!"

"No whining. You want the date or not?"

"If we're calling it a date, abso-fucking-lutely."

———

He picks me up from my exam and we head back to his place. He asks me how it went, and I launch into a too-long explanation of why I didn't like the exam questions, but I think I gave the answers the professor was looking for. My answer lasts all the way back to his place—which is nice, and I try to steer the conversation to that, but he just grins at me and asks another question about my exam.

He's been slowly unwinding from buttoned-up Scott as we've been talking. His tie came off—hot—and he unbuttoned his jacket—even hotter. Now he flicks open the top button of his dress shirt and I swear my panties get wet from that one simple action. "We can go out for drinks as soon as I get changed."

"You wanna go to the campus bar?" I ask, although really, I just want to help him get changed, and by that, I mean get naked. And then I want to ride him like a rodeo bronco. It is my celebration, after all.

He makes a face. "No."

I laugh. "Do you have a neighborhood bar around here?"

"Yeah." He watches me watching him slide off his dress

shirt. "Or we could get a bottle of tequila and a lime from the store and come back to my place. Or your place. Hell, we can call up your friends and invite them along."

"Seriously, I told you last night. Corey was my only friend. Being on an accelerated program made that kind of weird, because I stopped taking classes with the people I started with, and everyone else had already formed friendships. I mean, I'm friendly with people..." I'm babbling. I shake my head. "Don't worry about it."

Scott looks like he's torn between glowering and being sympathetic. He fails at the latter. Glower is in full effect. "We won't call Corey."

"He'll be so disappointed," I say, laughing as he roughly grabs my hips and slides our bodies together.

"I never wanted to get between you and a friend." He's serious about that, and I appreciate it.

I kiss his jaw. "I know. But if being reminded that I'm not interested steers him away, then maybe he wasn't that close of a friend to begin with."

"How the hell are you this mature? I still don't have that kind of objectivity."

"Yeah? What friends hurt you?"

Something flickers in his eyes, but I've learned that while I can ask that kind of question, and he'll never shut me down...he doesn't answer, either.

But it's my last day of school for a few weeks—until summer school begins, although I'll have some prep for that to do, because I'm finishing my senior project for double credit—and I don't want to go all emo about him not sharing when I've pushed for this to be light between us.

So I don't need to mess with feelings and secrets and heaviness. I've got a hot friend who wants to do tequila shots with me to celebrate my last exam of the spring. "Never mind. Bring it on, old man. Let's go get some tequila and see just how hard you can celebrate."

He grins at me, his white teeth glinting in the street light. "Famous last words, sweetness. Famous last words."

———

An hour later, we've got tequila and limes and salt—fancy salt that the fancy corner store in his fancy neighborhood sells for just this purpose.

And I'm a little drunk, obviously, because I'm adding fancy to every other word. Fancy that.

We're sharing life stories. His is considerably longer than mine.

I squint at him. "What happened?"

"I left the navy to join my father's company."

I frown, because that sounds...not fun. He gives me a bland look which just makes me wanna be sarcastic. Not my finest personality trait. I roll my eyes. "And now you're a bodyguard. That's a logical chain of events."

"It didn't work out. Although neither did being a bodyguard, so the common denominator there is me."

"But you liked the navy. And it sounds like the navy liked you."

"Yeah."

I don't ask for more than that. It's none of my business. But maybe we're not so different, Scott and me. I decide to share a little secret with him. Tequila makes me brave. "I've got one more semester left. Then I'm running away. I know Cole could find me anywhere, so like, not literally running away, but I'm done with my family. I want to go live somewhere they don't have a presence."

He gives me a long, perusing look. Like he's trying to figure out if I'm serious or if this is the fantasy of a college co-ed. "Where?"

I haven't figured that part out yet. "I don't know. Maybe London. Paris. Sydney, Australia sounds great."

He laughs. "You know other countries have rules about who can just move there, right?"

"You don't think the Queen of England wants me in her backyard? I'm not my sister. I'm not likely to blow a prince and leak the video."

"You better not." His jealousy is cute. Always nice to be wanted. But in this hypothetical-but-very-real fantasy of mine, I'm running away from Scott, too. I shift uncomfortably. "Ali," he growls, and I wave him off.

"Let's not talk about who I'm going to give future blow jobs to, okay?"

"Not okay." He tips me onto my back and crawls over me, tangling his hands in my hair as he crushes his mouth to mine. We make out like kids on his very nice rug for a few minutes, then I push him off me.

"I want another shot."

"Maybe we've had enough."

I give him a look. "Really?"

He snorts and pours me another shot. "Your funeral."

I'm warm and fuzzy, but I'm fine. I slam it back, then lick my lips and scoot back until I'm leaning against his couch. "Where would you go, if you could live anywhere in the world?"

"French Polynesia," he says without hesitation. "Most beautiful place on earth."

I nod. I've been to Tahiti once. "Nice."

"You don't agree."

I shrug. "Hard to take over the world from the middle of nowhere."

"That's my girl." There's legit pride in his voice as he says it, but this conversation just reveals the true divide between us. I want big cosmopolitan city, and a life of important responsibility. He wants...bikinis and no drama.

I fall silent, playing with a lime wedge.

"Let's not talk about you leaving. Or me...escaping to an island. That's just talk, you know."

"Okay." I don't want to talk about it, either. I meant to tell him that to share that I get how family can be fucked up, and it came out all wrong. Like I'll be flippant when what we have ends, and I won't.

I'll always remember Scott.

Always...

My stomach clenches hard at the thought of taking another man like I've taken Scott. It's unfathomable, really, but I thought losing my virginity would be this crazy thing, and it had turned out to be wonderful.

Maybe I'll be celibate once we part ways. I've certainly got enough fantasy fodder.

"Hey, smarty pants, stop that." I look up at him and he's holding out another shot. "One more, and then we take this party into my bedroom."

"Not right here?"

He grins. "I've got a nice big headboard. I want you to hold on to it while you ride my face."

Oh. My skin bursts into flames and I take the shot. "All right, then."

"I WANT to take you away for the weekend," I tell Ali, rolling onto my back. She slides against me, one of her thighs wrapping over mine. That's all it takes. One hot press of her naked body against mine and my cock is bouncing back to attention. She laughs quietly as he taps her leg, then sways up to my belly.

It's not fucking funny. I want back inside her. I want to mark her. Make her wet and stretch her to her max, so she's sore tomorrow and remembers who owns her pussy.

It's mine.

She's mine.

God, she's driving me out of my mind.

We need some time where I'm not working and she's not studying. Where we can touch and kiss and fucking consume each other, non-stop. So we can quench this insane fire that burns so bright between us, I can't even carry on a fucking conversation before rolling her onto her back and spreading her legs wide.

"I want to take you away for the weekend."

"We could just fuck for a weekend here."

I nip at her shoulder. "I need to go to London next week. Come with me to Europe. We'll go to Paris for the weekend, and then when we're in London, you can go shopping or study while I'm working."

"That's not taking me away for the *weekend*."

"But the weekend would be all ours. No interruptions. And then real life will intrude, as it always does, but at least we'll be together."

"Shopping?"

"There are Agent Provocateur shops in both Paris and London. In fact, there's one right around the corner from my flat."

"Your flat?"

"My apartment."

She hits me gently, but a flash of real hurt flickers across her face. Just for a second, and then it's gone. "I know what it means. Why do you have a *flat* in England?"

I rub my thumb over her cheek. "I lived there for two years. I thought it made more sense to buy a place than rent—turns out, that only makes sense to Americans. Their real estate system is a bit fucked up, and now I'm stuck with this place because I can't seem to sell it. My cousin stays there often, so it's not vacant, but she's also just as agreeable to not stay there should I need it for anything."

"You've got a cousin in England?"

I've got an entire English family, but I don't need to give her a genealogy chart. "Yeah."

"And do you..." She licks her lips, distracting me from the conversation, and I lower my head, tasting the wet trail she's just blazed. Her lip is soft and plump, and I pull it into my mouth. She groans and arches beneath me, but then she pulls away. "Stop it."

"I can't. I don't want to, either, so maybe I'm not trying hard enough, but you drive me crazy." I wrap my arms around her and roll onto my back.

Now she's on top. She's in control, and she wants to talk, she just needs to stay out of biting range.

"What was your question?"

She perches on my abs, her knees tucked together, her honey-brown waves spilling over her shoulders and hiding her breasts. Lady Godiva had nothing on Ali.

Innocent. Smart. Sexy as fuck.

And full of will-power and questions.

"Do you need it for anything?" She crosses her arms and gives me a stern look from on high.

"Next week I'm going to need it so we can play English Lord and his naughty maid."

She sticks out her tongue, then drops her hands to my chest. "More like...a proper young lady and the naughty butler."

Jesus. Yes. "Whatever you want."

"Okay. But I really need to work, so only a little bit of play."

I tug her down so I can kiss her. "I love how smart you are. My sexy fucking brainiac."

"Yeah?" She rubs her breasts against my chest and I groan. "Sexy?"

"Unbelievably sexy. When you take over the world, I want a full time job as your gigolo."

"You're hired," she whispers, raising herself up just high enough to capture my cock between her legs, the red, swollen head pointed toward me. She starts a slow, wet grind up and down my length. She likes this just as much as fucking.

"You want to see me come all over my stomach?"

She grins and nods.

"Such a cumslut."

A mock gasp turns her lips into a perfect O.

"Too dirty?"

"Hardly. Give it to me, old man. Come for me."

I've created a beautiful monster. I tip my head back and give in to the hot, slippery sensations as she demands and gets my release.

Booty Call

Ali and Scott

part three

LONDON

[21]

ALISON

MAY

PARIS WAS A NON-STOP SEXFEST. So I should be sore as we take the Eurostar train to London.

I *am* sore, and I've already told Scott that, but he's still worked his hand up my skirt and has me rocking against his fingers anyway.

I wasn't *too* sore. That's why I wore a skirt, after all.

"I love your pussy," he murmurs in my ear. "It's fucking juicy."

I blush.

"And I love that you get embarrassed about that."

"Just by the words," I mutter.

"And it makes you gush at the same time. Dirty girl."

My nipples tighten. How long until we get to his place? I thunk my head back against the seat and the guy behind us clears his throat. Damn it.

"Can't move," Scott whispers. "Still want my fingers?"

"Yes," I breathe back.

"Let's talk about your delicious pussy for a minute."

"Oh, God."

"Have you ever shaved it?"

"No."

"Would you?"

"Yes."

"You'd shave this pussy for me?"

I toss my head back and roll my hips, ignoring his instruction not to move. Fuck him. I want to come. "I'd shave it for me and let you enjoy it as a side benefit."

He laughs, but he tightens his arm. "And if I wanted you to shave it *for me?* Would you do that?"

Yes. In a heart beat. I swallow hard. "Maybe you should do it yourself. Make sure I'm completely smooth..."

I stretch the word out until it fades into a slow, hungry breath between us as I watch his face. He's curved around my body, blocking me from sight. I slide my hand between us and squeeze his cock. Two of us can play this torture game.

Except as soon as I start, he stops.

I pout.

He laughs. "Leave my dick alone and you can come," he whispers.

The blush crawls down my chest, towards my aching breasts, and I let him go.

"Good. When I get you to my place, I'm going to do just that, you know. I'm going to spread you out on my vanity and shave you bare. And then I'm going to lick you until you come on my face."

Scott loves going down on me. And I love it, too, but good Lord, can anyone hear him? I close my eyes as he slides two fingers deep inside me. He doesn't fuck them in and out of me. Instead he finds my G-spot and presses there, pulsing a bit as his thumb starts to work my clit.

"Did you know that the G-spot is the back of the clit?" he

asks, quiet as a mouse. I swallow a moan and shake my head. He makes a tutting sound with his tongue. "And you're such a smart girl. What are they teaching you at Georgetown?"

"Not that," I pant.

He presses his fingers apart, intensifying the feeling. "It's true. After I shave you, I'll do this again. Give you a *thorough* anatomy lesson."

"Awesome," I say, and he leans in closer, covering my lips with a soft, gentle kiss.

Then he flicks my clit, hard, with his thumb.

I moan and he swallows my cry. He does it again and I jerk. A third time pushes me over the cliff, sending me spiraling into a free-falling climax.

Twenty seconds later, the railway equivalent of a stewardess comes by and offers us warm towels for our hands. Scott takes them both with a straight face while I reconsider my question about sex killing me.

"You're so gorgeous when you come," he whispers as he hands over a towel.

Yes, definitely dying.

[22]
SCOTT

"You have...oh my God, look at that tub!"

It amuses me that a woman raised in the lap of luxury is impressed by the claw foot bathtub in my London flat. "It's deep," I murmur, enjoying the swell of her ass as she braces her hands on the edge of it and leans over, stroking the far side.

"You can't really buy tubs like this. I had a fancy soaker at my parents' estate, but nothing this legit. Holy crap." She groans as she straightens up. "I will be thinking about this tub all day."

"Not me?" I smirk at her as she turns around.

"Not hardly. You, I have at my beck and call back home. This tub... my affair with this tub is going to be a limited-time event."

And we aren't? But I know better than to ask her that. Because we are, one way or another, although we both want to push the inevitable end out as far as possible. And *not* asking questions like that is part of the dance.

We're not going to talk about what we aren't, what we can't be, because it's a given.

But what we *can be*... "I'll run a bath," I hear myself saying. "And move my meetings to tomorrow."

"Don't be silly," she says, but her eyes light up like it's Christmas.

And it's not silly. "When was the last time you had an entire day to yourself? No school work, no obligations?"

She presses her lips together. I suddenly realize the answer is her birthday weekend in New York, and I fucked that up for her, didn't I?

I pull my phone from my pocket and fire off a text message to my brother, who is at the Mayfair Enterprises offices here.

S: Just landed at Gatwick. Delays and now rush hour. Meet tomorrow?

It's not really a question, but I'm being courteous.

J: Fine. Swamped anyway.

I grin. "Out of the way, babe. I've got a tub to fill for you." I press up against her as she stands up and brush her hair to one side. I lower my lips to her ear. "I've got a fresh razor in the closet in the hallway. Go and fetch it like a good girl."

She shudders and I lazily spank her bottom. She presses against my palm.

While she's gone, I get naked and start to fill the tub. I add bubbles, which she squeals over when she comes back. I get in first, and she joins me, settling against my front, giving me free range to play with her boobs, which look amazing floating on top of the bubbles. She protests half-heartedly when I slide my hands lower and cup her pussy.

"Gentle," she reminds me.

My dick flexes at the memory of how many times we've fucked already this trip.

"I'll be good to her," I promise. "Super gentle."

She spreads her legs for me. I can't stop touching her, and not just her pussy. Every inch of her body is perfect to me, from her heavy breasts to her tight ass, and all the curves and long, lean limbs around them. She reaches back and tucks her hands behind my neck, arching her back.

I kiss one soapy arm, then turn and nuzzle behind her ear. She's got this sensitive spot there, and when I trace it with my tongue...

"Ahhhh!"

She grinds her ass back against me.

I grin. That gives me all sorts of ideas, but she wanted a bath. I'll give her that before I get dirty.

I sink lower into the hot, sudsy water, and she makes a little sound that punches me right in the chest. It's pure happiness. I want to bottle this moment for her. Maybe I'll have this tub ripped out and shipped across the Atlantic for her.

When she's boneless and blissed out, I nudge her to turn around in my lap.

She straddles me, finding my dick and giving him a happy little squeeze with her hands. "Who knew a bath would make me this happy?"

Not me. If I'd had half a clue, we'd have done this way sooner. "Come here," I whisper, my voice surprisingly hoarse.

She slips and falls into my chest, giggling as her lips seek mine out. Our kiss starts out lazy and silly, all lips and tongue and laughter, until she shifts on top of my erection and we notch together.

My brain short-circuits. We've done this once before, the first time, and I stopped myself.

Her breath huffs against my lips. Her eyes lock on mine. I'm a granite statue. This is her call.

"Just for a minute, maybe," she says, swivelling her hips in a mini-circle.

She's so slick. My cock is fucking begging for it. "Uhh-hh....God, Ali."

"Yeah." She's breathing so hard as water sloshes around us. "That's hot, huh?"

"Shit."

She lowers herself down, inch-by-inch, engulfing me in her heat.

I drop my head back and let my hands cup her breasts. Fucking perfect moment.

She goes slow, riding me up and down. Water's going everywhere and I can't get a good pinch on her nipples, she's slick and sudsy and it doesn't matter.

Fuuuuuck. I'm going to blow my load inside her. She's taking her fucking sweet time, and I'm going to fill her with come if she doesn't stop.

My head is swirling and my balls are practically drumming with excitement. Somehow—I have no fucking clue how—I manage to get my hands on her hips and stop her.

"Not yet," I say, not quite believing myself. "I promised to shave you."

She rocks in my lap. "But this is good, too."

"Good? This is perfect. But we agreed to talk about it, not just..." I groan and thrust into her. I twist one hand into her hair and give her my sternest face. "When I fill you with my come, it's going to be a deliberate fucking act. Got it?"

"So responsible," she teases, but she climbs off and balances herself on the corner of the tub, against the wall. As if she hadn't just scrambled all my brain cells, she lifts her legs and stretches them out along the sides of the tub. "So what do you want to do to me?"

I want to carry her to bed and do unspeakable things, but I'd promised other unspeakable things—that I really have no problem naming—so I shove my hungry dick back under the water and reach for the razor and shaving cream she'd procured from the closet.

I start by lathering myself up. She'd talked about wanting to watch me get myself off. This is just a variation on that, with shaving her in the middle.

"I don't like to shave everything off," I mutter, trying to watch her and keep working at the same time. "But I like having smooth balls."

She's staring at me, wide-eyed.

"Is this too dirty?" Jesus, what's wrong with me?

She shakes her head. "Too awesome. Not too dirty. Keep going."

I clean myself off, then sink into the water. "I thought I'd do the same for you. Leave your pretty curls on top, and shave the rest. It feels good."

"I bet," she breathes.

I squirt on a dollop of shaving cream and enjoy spreading it liberally over her mound and over her lips. I inspect my work area closely and decide to start on her mound, just above her clit, carefully shaving around a wide triangle of golden brown curls that would stay. Then with a few easy strokes, I bare her lips, pretty and pink and swollen. I press her open, doing a final swipe up the inside to catch any last strays, then scoop up some water with my hands and rinse her off.

She touches herself. "Oh," she says. "That's nice. That's... very, very nice."

I lean in and lick her fingers, her folds, her clit. I love my tongue over every inch of her delicious pussy, eager for more of her slippery juices. She leans back on her hands and her legs rise up out of the water. She's like a goddess in the surf, her tits jutting out and her tiny little waist nipping in, her legs bent and wide open for me.

I want her to come undone for me. I kiss her deeper, fucking her with my tongue as she grinds against my face. It gets me so fucking hard that I'm the only man who's ever done this to her. The only man who's felt her tighten like a coil, who's gotten to wind her up and taste her burst like a fucking peach.

Her juices are running down my face now, so fast I can't even swallow them, and in the tub below her I'm jerking myself off. She reaches her orgasm before I do, her thighs slamming tight around my head, and I keep her going until she pushes me away. Then I rear up, fisting myself as I rub my cock head all over her slippery cunt.

"In me," she whispers. "I just want to feel it."

She clings to me as I snap my hips and find home. My cock has to fight through her swollen folds, and I think it's gotta hurt her, but she's writhing against me, begging for more. She comes again, just like that—bam bam—and the slick pull does me in. An electric pulse starts in my balls and shoots through me. I pull out just in time and jerk my cock against her belly, shooting white ribbons of jizz all over her abdomen, and watch it drip down the crease between her hip and her thigh, onto her bare, silky pussy.

Before I can say sorry for being a dirty bastard or you're welcome, maybe, since she's whispering how good that was, she's pushing me back into the tub. She falls on top of me, laughing and kissing my mouth, long drugging kisses that would make me hard again if I had anything left in the tank.

"We're making a mess," she finally says, peering over the edge of the tub.

I don't fucking care. "Worth it," I mutter, squeezing her ass. "Best bath ever."

[23]
ALISON

We're heading out for dinner. Mostly because we need some fuel, but also because I've never been to England before, and I'd like to see more of it than just Scott's bathroom. And his bedroom, although all we did in there was nap.

Getting dressed reveals a neat side effect of being shaved— I'm super sensitive.

Scott grins at me as I shift while we wait for the elevator. *Lift*, I remind myself. I like all the different words. They're fun. England has shot to the top of my "run away from the family" destination list.

"Stop thinking about my bare pussy rubbing against my lace panties," I say under my breath. Then it's my turn to smirk. Ha.

"Stop giving me hard-ons in public," he mutters back.

We're hopeless. It's kind of gross, except that it's our secret and it's not gross between us. It's...I had no idea it could be like this. This kind of stupid-happy? This is what other people must mistake for love.

If I wasn't so jaded, I might do the same.

Good thing I'm totally cynical about such things.

The lift is old and creaky, and we joke about it, so when it stops with a bit of a bang and the doors open, I stumble out, giggling. Scott stops abruptly, and I right myself before looking around.

Ahead of us in the lobby is a woman.

She's beautiful. Blonde and aristocratic. Well dressed. We have the same boots, I notice. And she's staring at my boyfriend with a warm smile on her face.

I tell myself this isn't one of those times when everything I've started to let myself believe is proven to be a total lie—like the time I caught my mother sneaking into my grandfather's room in the middle of the night...or the time my oldest sister, who I idolized, gave the Vice President of the United States a blow job and filmed it for kicks...or the time my father murdered a call girl and got away with it—but I know this feeling.

I trust my gut. I'm twenty-fucking-years-old and I shouldn't be this wise to feeling like the floor is about to give way beneath me, but here it is.

Hello, betrayal, my old friend. I was wondering when you'd break my heart again.

Scott puts his hand on my arm. "Ali," he says, and I don't know if it's a warning or a plea.

"Scott," the woman says. "I didn't know you were back. I mean, I knew you *must* be returning, what with Jeff's new plans, and the expansion—"

"Madelyn." His grip on my arm tightens. "We were just heading out for dinner."

"Delightful!" She claps her hands together. "Could we join you?"

No, my heart hammers.

"Unfortunately our reservation is just for two," he says. It's a lie. We don't have a reservation. We don't even know where we're going to eat.

"Where are you going?" She gestures at the doorman

behind her. "I'm sure Jacques can call and convince them to move us to a table for four."

"Four?" Scott asks, and there's an edge there that confirms I'm not going to like the rest of the conversation.

Madelyn smiles. "John is just parking the car."

I dart my eyes back and forth between them. Who the hell is John?

"I see. Shame we'll miss him." Scott didn't sound like that was a shame at all. Since when did he lie through his teeth like a socialite on the dating circuit? "But we really must be heading off."

"No, no, it's fine." With a start, I realize that's me. Scott stares at me and I colour. "If you want..."

"Yes," Madelyn says, delighted. "Fine indeed!"

"It's *not* fine, Madelyn."

"Madelyn again?" She laughs. "Please, darling. Don't be all formal. I'm so glad that you are back." She moves in closer as she speaks, emphasizing *glad* as she presses her fingertips to the front of his shirt.

My head explodes. Or at least it feels like that, but since there isn't brain all over the antique everything in Scott's lobby, I guess that was just me not being able to cope with this porcelain doll come to life.

Touching my man like she knows him.

Because obviously, she *knows* him. And I don't know her, but then she turns to me, flashing green eyes curiously blinking out of that peaches and cream complexion, and she tilts her head to the side. "And you must be Alison."

My mouth drops open.

She knows me, too.

Well, fuck.

"Who are you?" I don't care if I'm being rude as I take a step back.

Her eyebrows raise just enough to confirm that yeah, I am.

Still don't care.

Scott crosses his arms and frowns at me as I move further away. It's a small lobby, I can't go that far, but he's still scowling at me. "This is Madelyn Dunn. I wasn't expecting to see her this trip. I apologize for not giving you a heads-up."

"A heads-up about what?"

"Honestly, Scott, must you always be so locked-up tight?" She smirks at me, like we're in on a joke together. But we're not. Hot, achy panic is settling into my chest, because I don't like that she knows all this stuff about Scott. I don't like that she assumes we're on the same level in that regard, and I'm pretty sure any second she's going to realize that actually, I don't know him nearly as well as she does.

And then I'm going to find out why that is.

I want to know, because fuck him for keeping secrets, but I don't want to know, because fuck me...I've fallen into caring about us. Valuing what we have, and now I don't know what that is.

What do we have?

Secrets, apparently.

And a beautiful British woman ready to spill them.

She smiles at me. "Scott and I were close once. We're still close, really."

I want to scream at her. Tell her to get her mitts off my man, but *they are still close* and we just have midnight hook-ups. And a single date with a tequila bottle. And this European adventure, although I'm starting to think that in the catalogue of our limited relationship, this might not fall into the relationship-building category.

I don't know anything about Scott and she knows everything, including why he's come back now and apparently what his business is.

My head hurts.

And she's still touching him. Her hand is wrapped possessively around his biceps and a vein throbs in my head as I stare at that point of connection.

I edge backward, nodding inanely.

Scott says my name, but it's like he's talking at the far end of a tunnel. Everything is fuzzy and echoing inside my head. My pulse is pounding in my throat and my eyes are itchy.

I know this feeling.

It's rare, because it's practically been bred out of me, but I'm going to cry.

Oh, no.

No, no, no, not effing happening, no.

Not going to cry over the guy who took my virginity. Nuh-uh.

He doesn't get that power.

I try to swallow. Oh, shit, that's hard. I try again, forcing the lump in my throat to move out of the effing way, because I don't have time to care.

I need to get my bag, find a cab, and get the hell out of this country.

"I forgot something upstairs," I say inanely and punch the button for the elevator. Lift. What-fucking-ever. The doors open and I stumble inside. There's no button to make it close faster, so I just stand there, face burning, as Scott glances back at me and talks faster at Madelyn.

I'm not listening. If I listen, I'll cry. If I cry, I'll lose my mind. So I think of Research Methods and try to guess where in the fourth floor stacks I'd find a book on quantitative data gathering, and *do not* think about the man I just realized I thought of as *my* man, and how fucked up that is.

How immature and pathetic I am.

Definitely not thinking about that.

Nope.

Quantitative data gathering. That's all that's on my mind.

And the doors close, just as Madelyn lifts her voice in my direction. "Really, genuinely lovely to meet you."

Nothing has sounded less genuine or lovely ever in the history of polite conversation.

[24]
SCOTT

I'm GOING to kill Madelyn.

"What the hell are you doing?" I demand, shoving her away from me. I need to go after Ali, but I need to know that Maddie won't follow, either. For all I know, she's got a key to my flat, and that's not on.

"Getting to know your...friend," she says.

"She's not just my friend and you know it. You're causing trouble. We are not close," I hiss under my breath. I don't need to make a scene in front of the porter, Jacques. "We weren't close when we were engaged, and we haven't spoken in more than a year."

She blanches. "I don't want someone taking advantage of you," she says stiffly. "That's all."

"If you know her name, then you know her family. Ali's the last person to take—you know what? It's none of your fucking business. Why are you really here?"

She frowns at me. "I live here."

What the *fuck?*

"John and I bought the flat on the second floor a few months ago. Evelyn didn't tell you?"

Evelyn is my cousin. Soon to be my dead cousin, if my rage has anything to say about it. She might be Maddie's best friend, but she's my fucking blood relation. "No."

"Oh, Scott." She sighs. "Go and smooth things over with your friend, and then come ring our bell. We'd love to catch up."

"Not happening. Change of plans, we're leaving tonight."

Her brow wrinkles. "I thought you were here to untangle your bank accounts? Such an unseemly mess, that."

"My cousin has a big mouth, and perhaps so does my brother. What I'm here to do is none of your business."

"It used to be my business."

"That was when you were going to be my wife," I growl at her. Behind me, I hear a gasp, and I turn around. Ali is standing there. I didn't hear the elevator.

She gives me a cold, level stare. "Change of plans, Mr. Mayfair. I'm heading straight to the airport. The full charge for our session can be paid directly to my pimp. An extra thousand for giving it to you up the ass."

Madelyn gapes at Ali as she sweeps past, and I'm tempted to laugh before I realize I need to stop her. I reach the street as Jacques, ever the efficient porter, already has a taxicab waiting for her.

I wave him off and grab the door. "Wait, babe..."

She swats at my arm. "Fuck you, Scott. You think I'm over-reacting? I was fucking falling for you. You know that? That's what I realized in the elevator as we came down to the lobby. I was thinking, holy fuck, this is something special. And then I find out...nope, you're nothing special. You're a giant dick, full of secrets and lies. Which is fine and dandy if we're just fucking, which is what I wanted in the first place, but you had to go and worm your way into my heart. That's off-limits. I'm going home, and you can't stop me. I don't want you to try. I don't want you to do anything, you get me?"

"No." I ignore the driver, who's shooting daggers at me, either for holding up his fare or more likely for taking advantage of a young woman, and I lean into the cab. "I didn't tell you about Madelyn because it's embarrassing, nothing more. And the rest of it is just nothing. It's the boring shit. You're right, we've got something between us—"

"No we don't. That was a lie. A fantasy like everything else." She turns to the driver. "Can you call the police? The bobbies? Whatever you call them. I want this man away from me."

"Whoa, stop." I shake my head. "You are way overreacting here."

She glares at me. "Get out of my fucking cab. Is that woman your ex-fiancée? Did you forget to tell me that you'd been engaged? Does she know more about you than I ever will? Get. Out. Of. My—"

I back up. "Okay." I pull out my wallet and hand over a hundred pounds to the driver. "Take her—"

"I can tell him where to take me," she snaps. "Get out."

Numb with disbelief, I step away from the car and close the door. I need to follow her, but I also need to meet with my brother and do something about my bank accounts and not get arrested for harassing a woman right after I've just been let back in the country.

Heading back inside, I find the lobby mercifully empty. I'm shaking with rage by the time I get to my flat. It takes me three minutes to pack my bags and head back downstairs.

Jacques, having read my mind, has another taxi waiting. I give him a couple of folded bills and thank him for his help. Then I get in the cab and give the driver my brother's office address.

[25]

ALISON

THE DESK CLERK at the airport hotel doesn't blink when I ask to be registered under a pseudonym. Maybe this is how celebrities do it. I hand over my credit card, grateful for the privilege that allows me to not sleep at the airport tonight—that allows me to flee to the airport, passport in hand, knowing that I can just buy the next available flight home.

I don't cry until I'm behind the locked door of my hotel room, and even then, I wait until I'm in the shower to really let loose.

Doubt is already warring with anger inside my heart. Should I have stayed and heard him out?

Is there anything he could say to make this okay?

He's watched my family dynamic. He knows how wary I am.

If I'm not going to put myself first and protect my heart, how can I ever expect a man to do the same? No. I need to leave.

But as I towel off and curl up on the bed, I already miss him. I miss his laugh, and how big he is when he wraps around me. I miss his arms, holding me tight, and I miss the lie that I'd started to believe was blooming between us.

That's the fucking kicker.

Even as I tell myself it was a fantasy concoction, I miss it so much it feels like a knife cleaving me in two.

I fall asleep, but my phone wakes me up while it's still dark. My flight isn't until midmorning. I grab at it, heart pounding. If it's Scott, will I answer? Will I be able to stop myself from answering?

Fingers shaking, I lift it so I can see the screen.

It's Hailey.

My heart cracks again.

When I don't answer, she texts.

H: Scott called me. He said you had a fight. Setting aside the fact that I didn't know you two were together...are you okay?

A: We're not together

H: Awww, sweetie, I'm sorry

A: Nothing to be sorry about, it's fine

H: You're in England

A: Leave it alone

H: Okay

A: I might need to hide at your place for absolutely no reason

H: We'll pick you up, let me know what time your flight gets in

I send her the details and turn off my phone. I don't want to stay with my sister, really, but I can't go home. Scott will come there sooner or later, and I'm not sure I'm strong enough to ignore him.

[26]

SCOTT

Jeff stares at me across his massive desk. "You want me to do what?"

"You don't need to do it yourself. Just get someone to do it." I've given him a list of tasks I need taken care of here in England. I'm leaving for Washington on an afternoon flight. Ali's on a morning flight, which I couldn't get on, no matter how big the bribe. It's bad enough that I can't get there to be waiting for her. I'm not losing another day or two just to handle some basic administrative details.

"You want a bathtub removed from your flat and shipped to the U.S."

"Yes."

"They sell bathtubs back home. Not sure if you're aware."

"Humor me." And it's the only part of my flat I care about anymore. If a flame thrower could be taken to the entire building, that would make me happy.

"Fine." He glances at the rest of the list. "You'll need to provide our attorneys with an affidavit allowing them to act on your behalf with the banks."

"We can do that over breakfast."

He scowls. "I take it this means you aren't coming to see the nanotechnology lab tomorrow." We were going to take a helicopter up to Leeds. I thought Ali would enjoy it.

Acid rises in my throat at the damage my secrets caused her. "Not this time."

"Shame. When we begin the process to go public with Mayfair Enterprises, I'm going to buy the lab from the company. I'd enjoy bringing you into this new venture."

"Not my dream, bro."

"Fair enough." He rocks back in his chair. "I really didn't tell Madelyn anything, you know."

I don't know if I can believe him or not. I do know he didn't hurt me on purpose, but my brother can be thoughtless. Selfish.

Apparently it's a family trait.

"Not really my priority right now." I press my thumb against the throbbing vein in my temple. "How long until we can rouse one of your lawyers from bed?"

"You should get some sleep yourself."

"Not an answer."

"I can get them up now if it's that important."

Has he not been fucking paying attention? "It's that important."

He picks up the phone. I don't miss the eye roll. I don't care.

An hour later, three lawyers are in the boardroom with me, listening to the entire clusterfuck tale of my investigatory role when I was here last, how I was found out by John Glandsworth while he was sleeping with my fiancée, accused of spying on the government, and run out of the country with my tail between my legs because of my family name.

"And why wasn't this...taken care of two years ago when the dust-up occurred?" one of them asks me.

A dust-up. I was a fucking spy, and because of my family's

wealth, it's no big deal. "I didn't want any favors from my father."

From the corner of the room, where he's been writing on his tablet, Jeff snorts. "But from your brother…"

I didn't want to owe him, either. "Desperate times and all that."

"I can't believe all it took to bring you back into the family fold was a woman."

"I wouldn't say I'm back in the fold."

"Then why did I summon Mayfair family solicitors—"

The lead lawyer cleared his throat. "Barrister."

"Whatever," Jeff waves his hand, and it reminds me painfully, blindingly of Ali talking about the different words the Brits use for things.

She'd been having such a good time. All her guards were down. She'd thought she'd flown halfway around the globe and away from her toxic family, and when she wasn't looking, my own toxic history hissed in her face.

I'd wanted to protect her, and I ended up hurting her terribly.

"Fine. I owe you one. Now can we get this over with? I need to get to the airport."

By mid-morning, I've signed a dozen legal documents and arranged to put my flat up for sale again. This time, an agency will deal with all the details, and coordinate with a solicitor in the legal firm's offices.

Jeff promises his assistant will keep him apprised of everything so I don't need to think about it again, and asks me to have lunch with him again in New York sometime soon. "You owe me," he reminds me.

"Lunch it is." The promise rolls off my tongue more smoothly than I expect. Maybe these baby steps of leaning on him for help are actually working to bridge a connection again.

Terrible to think that it's easier because the old man has passed on, but that might just be the truth.

Too complicated a truth to worry about now, though.

I've got a plane to catch.

A woman to find.

And a fight to finish.

Booty Call

Ali and Scott

part four

WASHINGTON, AGAIN

[27]

ALISON

It takes Scott three days to talk his way past Cole and Hailey. By the time he does, he's pissed. "Ali!" he hollers as he stomps into their living room. "Get your ass out here and stop hiding from me."

"I'm not hiding," I snap as I slide out of their guest room, although yeah, that's exactly what I was doing. "I just didn't want to see you."

I'm not ready for this, but he's made his point. He's not going away until we hash this out more than what I yelled at him in the street outside his flat.

I flush with embarrassment at the memory of how I acted. I'm not proud of having let his ex get under my skin like that.

And despite my anger, and my regret, my first reaction when I catch sight of him is my heart leaping into my throat.

He looks like hell. He hasn't shaved. Probably hasn't slept, either.

He looks like he needs a hug, and Cole sure as shit isn't going to give him one. My brother-in-law is standing toe-to-toe with Scott—so he's been allowed in, but he's on a short leash.

I'm not going to give him a hug, either, I don't think, but I don't need a pit bull protecting me either.

"Cole, can you give us the room?"

He gives me a surprised look and I shrug. I might not be happy with the guy, but he's not going to hurt me.

I settle on the couch and gesture to the chair across from me. He takes it, his gaze wary at my sudden adoption of social niceties. "What? I went to finishing school."

"I know," he said slowly, a faint hint of a smirk curling at the corner of his lips. It's maddening how much I like his face. I don't want to like any part of him, but especially not the part that lied to me and won me over. And the part that watched me, carefully, learning me inside out when I wasn't given the same privilege. "But you hate that part of yourself, and glory in being a little inappropriate. Or, when pissed off, a lot inappropriate."

I narrow my eyes at him. "Pissed off for a legit reason."

He nods. "Yeah."

"What do you want, Scott?"

"I want to talk. Air what needs to be aired, and get this behind us."

"So talk."

He shifts uncomfortably. "What do you want to know?"

I huff a frustrated breath. "How am I supposed to know that? How about the complete, unvarnished truth of who you are?"

"That's complicated."

"Well, it turns out I'm not that complicated. So...nice knowing you."

"Whoa, wait." He holds out his hands, palms up, fingers spread. "Stop making snap, rash decisions like that."

I frown, adrenaline ricocheting through my body. I try to ignore the fight or flight reflex pressing hard against my ribcage from the inside out. "This isn't going to work if you tell me how to be."

"How will it work?"

"I don't know."

"But it will, if we figure out a way?" It's so easy to hear hope in his voice. To listen to the matching voice streaming through my mind, chanting that I can trust him and if I just crawl into his lap, it'll all be okay.

I can't trust that voice.

I can't trust him.

I shake my head. "I didn't mean to promise that. I don't know."

He moves forward, settling right on the edge of his chair. He's fisting his hands so tightly his knuckles are white. "I don't want to push you, Ali."

I stare at his hands and my frown deepens. "I don't think that's true. I think you're barely holding yourself back from grabbing me and shaking me and telling me I'm wrong."

He makes a frustrated sound but doesn't deny it. He gets a point for not denying it.

I stand up. "Come back tomorrow. Bring cupcakes."

———

He brings a half-dozen chocolate cupcakes.

I look in the box and burst out laughing. Hailey leans closer, then looks up in confusion. "Ali doesn't like chocolate."

I nod, my gaze locked on Scott's the whole time. "And Scott doesn't like to be told what to do."

He stares right back. "But I'm here."

I shrug. "Tomorrow, bring me lemon ones and we'll talk."

———

There are three lemon cupcakes the next day, and we sit on the couch together, the cupcakes between us, for nearly an hour.

His beard is getting pretty long. I want to rub my hand over it and find out if it's soft or prickly. I can't decide which I'd rather.

I settle for asking about the "work" he didn't get to do in England.

"My brother..." he trailed off. "Do you know I have two brothers?"

I do now. I've done the complete Google search on him I should have done months ago. "Yeah."

"Jeff extended the use of Mayfair attorneys to me. I was already using them on this end to smooth over some immigration difficulties I was having, so...basically I took advantage of having them at my disposal and they're going to..."

"To....what?"

He looks at me like I'm an idiot.

I throw my hands in the air. "I don't know what you do, Scott! You're not just a bodyguard, remember? All mysterious and shit?"

He has the good graces to look chagrined at least. "Right. It's...complicated."

I roll my eyes. "Well, great."

"What do you want from me?" he asks.

"I don't know," I mutter. "Maybe what I want is something you can't give me."

We fall into a frustrated silence for a bit, then he asks me about my project. I've done fuck all on it, but I let myself talk about my plans. It's not a real conversation, but it's something.

When we fall silent again, I twist so I'm looking at him more full-on, and I tuck my feet under my butt.

"Are you cold?" he asks.

"No. Yes." It's actually a pretty hot day out there, but I'm suddenly chilled.

He passes me a soft blanket from the end of the couch. Our fingers brush against each other briefly and my heart hammers against my chest, like, let me out of here, because my rightful place is over there. I ignore it and wrap the blanket around myself, but from the stricken look on Scott's face, he's having a similar reaction.

Well, then we're both fucked, aren't we?

I'm suddenly snappish. I pin a hard stare on him. "What do you want?"

He answers terrifyingly quickly. "I want you back."

My mouth goes dry. "That scares the living daylights out of me."

He nods, the corners of his mouth turning down.

"I think...I'm just too young, you know? I'm not meant to..." Fall in love, that's what I want to say here, but I can't. I can't show him that again. I did once, in England. I yelled it in anger, and now he's latched on to it like it might be the thing that brings us back together.

It's not.

"I'm not meant to get attached yet. And that I did, and it went badly...that's a poor reflection on me."

He shakes his head. "No. I ended up being your worst nightmare, and that was preventable. It won't happen again."

I know it won't. I'll never risk it again. "Thank you for bringing me cupcakes," I say quietly. "Two days in a row, even."

"My pleasure."

"You should go now."

It takes him a minute to realize I'm dismissing him. "No. Don't do this."

"It's not you..." I say, trailing off, but it is. He's too much for me. Too old, too serious, and carrying too much baggage. "It's just that I can't handle all that a relationship would demand."

He glares at me. "Now who's the liar?"

I jut my chin out at him. "Get out."

"This isn't over."

"Of course it is. Not everything happens at your beck and call."

He scowls at me. "No. It happens at yours."

"Screw you."

His arm snaps out and he strokes my cheek, then rubs his thumb across my lower lip. "Anytime you want, babe. Anytime you want."

WHEN I LEAVE Ali that afternoon, I mean to go home. But I swing past The Horus Group offices and Wilson's doing his creepy stalker thing again. Jason growls at him that it's inappropriate and Tag suggests we all go out for a liquid lunch.

This is how we wind up weaving down Connecticut Ave right around the time that everyone else is leaving work. We're probably taking up too much space on the sidewalk, but who's going to tell us to get out of the way?

We really just need to get to the other side of Dupont Circle. Then we can dump ourselves on the Metro and head home to our beds.

Except Wilson. He claims he's going back to the office.

Lunatic.

"I don't even want to work anymore," I say out loud, to nobody in particular.

A woman walking buy snorts. "Of course you don't," she mutters.

"Hey!" I call, spinning around. "I served this country!"

"Shut up," someone else says, and I'm going to make another

smart remark when I realize it was Jason. He's shaking his head at me. "Don't use that as an excuse."

"It's not an excuse," I mumble. Fuck, I'm wasted. And it's not true that I don't want to work. I do. I just don't know what I want to do, exactly. "It's a *fact*."

"It's also a fact that leaving the navy was your own free fucking choice, asshole, so get over yourself."

He's got me there.

I shrug. "Yeah."

"We should eat something," Tag says, rubbing his stomach. "Steak, maybe."

The hostess at the steakhouse we go into gives us a dubious look, but she seats us in a booth in the back, and by the time we've eaten senator-sized dinners, we're all more or less sober. Not driving sober, but good to make it to the subway station.

I'm just upright enough to think that texting Ali is a good idea. Nobody else is sober enough to stop me.

S: I miss you.

She doesn't reply. I stare at our messages all night, and for the next week, until I get drunk again with Wilson and delete the entire history.

I still miss her like fucking mad. But she doesn't miss me at all, and that's all there is to it.

Can't get blood from a stone.

Can't get love from a broken girl.

I know there's something wrong with that thinking, but I'm too wound around the axle to see it any other way.

[29]
ALISON

S: I miss you.

I READ this text message every single morning and every single
night for two weeks.

It breaks my heart every single time, because my fingers
ache to tap out the truth. *I miss you, too.* I don't send anything,
though, because the rest of the problem—that I really can't
handle how much he wants from me, how much I feel for him
despite myself—remains true.

Every night, my body betrays me by dreaming of him.
Erotic, filthy imaginings. Sometimes it's what we did
together. Sometimes it's even more depraved acts we never
got to. He ties me down and works me up until I'm
begging him to take my ass. He spanks me until my
bottom is black and blue. He makes me blow him in
public.

That's the most recurring dream, the public humiliation,
and I'm sure a therapist would have a field day with my guilt for
exploding at him in London, and how far my dream self is
willing to go to make that up to him.

I'm more fascinated by the disturbing reality that my real self isn't willing to do much at all.

When my thoughts wander in that direction, I force myself to get to work on my research. What's done is done, and if I'm really that brutal, then I can be matter-of-factly mind-over-matter about it and move on.

It's an early morning in June when he texts next.

S: Shameful admission: I deleted the history of our text messages.

I gasp when I read that. And where nothing else before worked, this has me firing back a reply before I think about it.

A: Oh no. Whatever will you wank off to now?
S: Secret videos I took of you. Sleeping. Other things.

I laugh out loud. It fades to a bittersweet sigh when I realize that, yeah, that's definitely just a joke, and not for a second do I feel any panic about the implied threat.

A: If you ever want to see any of the dirty texts I sent you, I've still got the complete record
S: Is that a sideways booty call?
A: You want it to be?
S: No
S: Do you want it to be?
A: Maybe

As soon as I send it, I'm squirming in my chair. Damn it. That was not how that was supposed to go.

But it was still pretty hot.

S: Let me know if it gets desperate over there

A: That's selfless of you

S: Your orgasms have always been my top priority

He's kidding.
I'm kidding.
Right?

———

Another week goes by, with a few more text exchanges. And I never intend to actually suggest he come over, until I'm up late one night and the squirming in my chair gets to the point where I'm thinking about heading to bed with my phone.

Damn it. If I'm going to do that, I might as well invite him over.

This is a terrible idea.
Definitely a mistake.

A: You busy?

His response takes just long enough that I start to worry about where he is at ten thirty at night.

S: Depends.

A: Wanna come over?

[30]

SCOTT

I HAVE no idea why I'm letting her suck me back in.

I know she doesn't want anything other than ex-sex, and I'm gonna be pissed about this at some point down the road.

It doesn't stop me from heading over to her place anyway.

When she opens the door, it's a punch in the gut how great she looks. She's wearing sweatpants, low on her hips, and a girly t-shirt that skims her curves. Casual and fuckable and perfect.

"You summoned me?" I stalk past her before she gives me an answer.

Behind me, she lets the door swing shut. "Is that how it's going to be?"

I pace into her kitchen. The overhead light is off, but the hanging pendants over the peninsula are on, casting warm light on the center of the room that quickly fades to dark corners.

It's quiet and intimate, and I have to fight to keep my angry edge. It would be so easy to just let this happen.

I roll up my shirt sleeves as I turn to look at her. I catch her eyeing up my forearms and I flex those muscles for her. "So where do you want to fuck?"

"That's not—"

"No, that's exactly what you want from me. And all you want from me. I'm a cock at your pleasure tonight."

Her eyes flare at me. "Not just a cock. I like your fingers and tongue, too. Sometimes even more."

"More?" I loom over her and she sucks in a ragged breath. Does she smell my body wash and after shave? Is she thinking about the fact that as soon as she texted me, I threw myself in the shower?

I'm at her mercy here.

I love/hate that.

"Equally," she says quietly, her gaze cautious now.

"No, you said more. You don't love my cock enough to get fucked tonight, Ali."

"We don't need to fuck." She stumbles over the word and I hate myself for pushing her. She stands tall and smirks, proving once again I've underestimated her. "Wanna play Little Big Planet?"

I laugh. Funny girl. "No."

"What do you want to do?"

I walk her back until she bumps against the counter. At the same time, I settle my hands on her hips. Hot and heavy, I hold them there, my fingers squeezing the top of her ass, my thumbs rubbing lazy circles on her hip bones.

She feels incredible.

She feels fragile.

She feels like mine, and nothing less than that will do.

My jaw flexes as I glare down at her. "Sunday brunch."

"No!" The protest rips out of me first of all because it's only Tuesday, and the last thing I want is him to turn around and head out the door until Sunday. And I'm still pissed at him about all the secrets, so I'm not giving him a date.

Not yet.

But he probably thinks I'm saying no for other reasons.

He's not wrong. Dating would open a Pandora's box of mess that we could avoid by...not dating. On the other hand, *not dating* didn't work out that well for us either. I'm not stupid. I know that any way we do this, it's going to be messy.

Evidence: right now. He's pissed, and I'm not climbing him like a tree right now, getting that blissful orgasm I want so bad.

Which is really his fault, anyway. "You know, this whole thing is a monster of your own making," I point out, trying to pull us back to the light flirting of our text messages.

Yes, I summoned him.

Yes, I texted him late at night because I want his cock inside me. I can't fall asleep without the hard press of his body against mine, his words in my ear as he growls all the filthy ways I turn him inside out.

I need him, plain and simple.

We also need to talk, but I keep forgetting that as I watch his forearms flex and twist. Corded muscles popping out of the shadows, golden bands of strength that make my mouth water.

I set my hands against his chest. He doesn't move. I sigh and stroke his curved pecs, then slide my fingers together, meeting in the middle. I play with the buttons there. He's still just staring down at me. "I had no idea how awesome sex was until you showed me. If you don't want me to text you…"

I trail off, because I'm not going to make an empty threat. I'm not calling anyone else, and I can't even pretend I'm not going to call him, either.

"I'll trade you," he finally says. "Dates for orgasms."

I laugh. "I'm going to get the orgasm anyway. You're even worse at this lying thing than I am."

He sighs as he winds one hand into my hair, tipping me back just a bit. Trapping me at just the right angle to crash his mouth down on top of mine.

As our tongues slide against each other, as he fills my body, sweeping all my defences away like they're made of air, I think… what am I fighting, really?

So he's broken my heart.

He'll probably do it again.

So what.

It'll be worth it.

But then he pulls back, nipping at my bottom lip as he separates us back into two people, and he says, "Fine, then. Dates for secrets."

And *whoosh*, my defenses are back in place. Because there aren't enough date possibilities to trade for all that remains unspoken between us. I wrap my arms around myself and shake my head. "You know you won't really do that."

"You don't think I'll bare my soul to you?" He steps back

and spreads his arms wide. He looks like an avenging angel, his dark hair flopping over his hooded gaze, his hands turned skyward. Tall and lean and wide and mean.

"I think there's room for you to bare plenty and still not really tell me anything at all. I think that you and I use the word secrets in two totally different ways."

His head lifts up an inch, and his eyes glitter. "You need to get over what happened in London."

"And you need to not speak to me like I'm a child."

"I'm here, aren't I?" He growls. "Even when it's only a fraction of what I want, I'm here because you snapped your fingers."

I gasp. "That's not fair."

"No? You don't think I'm yours?"

"I think you were someone else's first, in so many more ways than you'll ever be mine."

"We can't all be virgins, Ali. You might not have been my first, but you're my last. My only."

I shake my head. "Don't say that."

"You don't want to know how much you mean to me? You don't think I'll fight for you? I'd kill for you. If I back off, it's only to regroup."

"You're going about it all the wrong way," I cry, frustrated he doesn't see it as clearly as I do. "All you have to do is be honest with me!"

"It's not that simple," he grinds out. "You say that like I know what you want to hear, but I don't have any clue. You want to know...what? Do you want me to be honest about my kill count in war zones?"

"Fiancées would be a good start."

"Fine. I had one. It was a mistake."

"Do you not hear yourself? I'm banging my head against a brick wall here. You had two chances already. I've already told you my darkest secrets. I told them to you before you even had a piece of me. So don't tell me that I don't know what you're holding back. I *know*, Scott. Because I've given you my soul. Fuck this *baring it* nonsense. You *own* my soul. So no, I don't want to give you my heart, as well, because I still don't have *anything* of yours. See how telling me a bit here and there won't make that *fucking even?*" I'm raging now, so hard that I'm shaking, and suddenly he's got me in his arms.

"I'm sorry." They're simple words, and they don't actually say much. But it's the way he says them, gruff and rough, emotion scratching each round syllable until the two words are burrs that hook into me and hang on. "You did, and I didn't, and it's not enough. I'll do better."

I shake my head. "I don't want...I don't want promises."

He's holding me so tight now that it hurts. "What do you want?"

I want this. "You. Just you."

He presses his forehead against mine. Our noses jostle for position as we kiss each other. It's fast and furious, a little rough and a lot raw, but it feels right.

It feels right, too, when he wrenches down my pants, all the way to my ankles, and sets me on the kitchen counter. Eyes dark and burning, he strokes the seam of my pussy. "You've been shaving."

"Just tonight. For you."

He jerks my hips right to the edge of the counter and drops to his knees, shoving his face right between my legs. There's nothing smooth about this. He's hungry for me, and I'm dying for any touch on offer. The combination is combustible, and it doesn't take long before I feel an orgasm start to build deep in my belly.

But he's not going to give it to me that easy.

My orgasms are his to dole out, and he's going to make me

work for them. If he can't trade something else, he'll just trade in this—my ache, my need.

I don't blame him. I'd do the same thing in his shoes.

He stands again, his hands rough and insistent on my hips as he slams our bodies together. I taste myself on his face. It makes my legs shake.

He looks down between us as he licks his lips. "You're wet," he says. Understatement.

"You turn me on," I admit plainly.

He shakes his head. "It's not me. It's you. You're pure passion, Ali."

I can't imagine ever sharing that with anyone else. "Just with you."

He gives me a sad smile. "I know."

He touches me, stroking me at first, then he slides a finger and then two fingers inside, making me stretch both around him and for him. I love his fingers. I'd told him, hadn't I?

And he'd told me I didn't deserve his cock.

My face flames.

"What are you thinking about?"

"You said I can't have your cock."

He gives me a long, appraising look. "That's right. That was harsh."

"Your fingers are enough," I pant.

"Yeah?"

I nod. "But I want more." And the flame burns brighter.

He adds a third finger. I know this because he tells me, but I'm not watching anymore. It's too much. Too dirty.

It's perfect.

The stretch this time turns into an ache before he's all the way inside me, but he does that thing, a flick or a flutter, deep inside me, and it lights me up. I spread my legs wider still— obscenely so, now, but I don't care, because this feels too good.

My ankles tangle together in my pants and I kick them free, lifting my heels up to the counter. I'm spread wide open for him now.

"Can you take another?"

I nod. Words aren't possible right now, because all I can think about is that warm pressure inside me, that rub and then—oh God—another flick. I cry out and bear down against his hand, and he eases back.

"No, no, no," I pant. "More."

He's leaning over me now, his eyes locked on mine. "More?"

Another nod, and he's sliding back into me. This time the stretch starts almost immediately, but he still finds that spot. I breathe out, not a word, exactly, but it sounds something like *ohmygod* and *you'reagod*, and both sentiments are true. He's figured out my body like I never thought possible, and even though I've been such a bitch to him, he gives me this.

Flick.

I gasp and arch my back, sliding another quarter inch onto his hand.

"You are the most beautiful woman in the world," he growls at me. "Fucking exasperating, but beautiful, and hot, and even when you're pissed at me, you give me this."

I give *him* this? I'm really sure I'm not giving anything right now.

I'm taking a hell of a lot.

He groans as he twists his hand, and I feel it—a spark like never before. It's slow, so slow I don't even recognize it as a building toward something at first. I just think, wow, that feels impossible. And impossibly good, too. But then he pulses his fingers out, then in again, and he's only moving the tiniest bit, but now that spark is brighter. And it's growing. Like watching a charge lit far, far away, I sense the orgasm coming before I really *feel* it build, but when it hits it's like a freight train of physical sensation.

Whoosh. Blood rushes through my head as he fucks his hand in and out, in and out, and I reach blindly for my clit. When I touch it, I realize I'm *soaked*. Like never before.

Scott's got four fingers, maybe even five, inside me, and I'm gushing slippery fluid like...nothing I can... "Oh," I cry out. That's it, a single sound. *Oh.* My body shatters into separate elements. Sound: loud, scary. Light: bright and all-encompassing. Touch is weird, because I float out of my body for a minute, so I can't feel anything, and then I can feel *everything*. The wetness between my legs. The empty, yearning ache as Scott picks me up and carries me to bed. He holds me close and tells me I'm beautiful as he rolls on a condom, then fills that emptiness inside me, stretching me in the most delicious way until I'm coming again. He explodes right after me.

When he gets us under the blankets, I burrow into his chest and hope that when I snap back to reality, I can find the words to tell him I love him.

I love him and need him, no matter how fucked up I am.

[32]
SCOTT

I don't think one intense night is going to fix everything in
our relationship.

I'm hoping croissants and lemon curd might help, though, so
I'm holding Ali to my request for Sunday brunch.

Of course, that's five days after she invites me over, and I fill
the intervening days with as many orgasms as she wants—gotta
keep her happy to distract her from the fact that we're sort of
dating again.

After Paris, I've missed sleeping with her, and this week I
haven't spent a single night in my own bed.

I'm pretty fucking happy about that, and Ali seems to like
it, too.

Heading to Eastern Market on Sunday, though, she's wary.
Hence the lemon curd.

It's going to be my secret weapon.

"Do you need coffee?" I ask her as we pick our way through
the outdoor market.

"I've got coffee."

"But do you have Jamaican Blue coffee?"

"Does that make a good vanilla latte?"

Jesus. "What did you say I drink? Boring old man coffee? This is the best of the best of boring old man coffee."

"No vanilla syrup?"

"You won't need it."

She gives me a skeptical look and I grin and pay the man.

She stops and points her finger at me. "I thought you wanted to go out for brunch? You're buying everything we need for a breakfast at home."

I shrug. "I think I just said brunch. I didn't specify where."

"Interesting," she says, looking at me suspiciously.

"Is it?"

"Hmmm. Very."

"Good. I like to be interesting to you." I offer her my arm and she takes it. "Raspberries?"

"Sure. After we have brunch, are you going to go back to your place and see if it's still standing?"

"Have I been at your place that long?"

"A few days."

"Is that a problem?"

She doesn't answer right away. So prickly, my Ali.

"Maybe we should take this stuff back to my place to eat," I say, not looking at her. It's hard not to blurt out everything I want. How I've got her bathtub coming all the way from England, although that might have to go into storage for a while. How I'd do anything to make her happy. I swallow that down and pretend I could let her go again. "That way you could escape whenever you want."

"I don't want to escape." She says it quietly, but it lands squarely and I puff like a peacock.

"No?"

"Not today, anyway."

"K. Good."

[33]
ALISON

I WAKE up a week later to an empty bed. It's such a rare occurrence now that my first thought is, "Where's Scott?" in genuine confusion. It's a good kind of weird.

My second thought is that I really want some of that damn coffee he bought. Then I realize that's because I can smell it coming from my kitchen. But when I get there, I just find the freshly brewed coffee with a note explaining that he's headed to the Mayfair Enterprises offices in Maryland for "boring corporate stuff."

I roll my eyes and pour myself a cup of coffee, breathing it in before I pad to the fridge for the milk.

It's good, but it's still coffee. It needs a healthy splash of dairy.

Attached to the milk carton is another note, this one telling me to check my email. He's drawn goofy smiley face with a body...and a raging boner.

Classy.

I'm still giggling as I search the living room for my phone. I think I may have shoved it somewhere when we were getting busy last night.

I find it under a cushion and check my messages. Twenty minutes earlier, Scott sent me an email with a couple of attachments. The first one is a scan of his medical test results. The second is a sworn affidavit—oh my God, he's such a dork—signed by Wilson Carter as a witness.

My heart pounds in my chest as I read his sworn statement.

I, Scott Mayfair, do solemnly and faithfully attest to the fact that I have only had sexual relations with one woman, Ms. Alison Dashford Reid, since December of 2014.

I blink at the screen. 2014?

I pick up the phone and tap his name on my screen. He answers on the first ring and I launch into it before he has a chance to say anything. "You haven't slept with anyone else in like *a year and a half?*"

"Well, you haven't slept with anyone else, ever."

"That's different."

He laughs. "How so?"

"I didn't know how amazing sex was. Not truly. It was an academic notion."

He grunts. "It wasn't an academic notion while we were broken up."

"True. But...you know." I can't imagine ever wanting to have sex with anyone else.

"What?"

"Shut up, that's what."

"So you accept my documentation?"

Of course I did. "I suppose."

"I love it when you play hard to get."

I snicker.

"I can be back in the city in four hours."

That sounds perfect. Except…"Damn it!"

He laughs. "Oh no, what?"

"I've got a meeting with my advisor this afternoon."

"Okay. Dinner, then."

"Dinner and sex, so classy. It'll need to be late."

"Late is my speciality. We can make it pizza for that special touch."

I chuckle. "And eat it in bed."

———

First rule of teasing in a new relationship: know what your hard limits are.

I stare at Scott as he plops the pizza box in the middle of my bed.

"No?" he asks, and it's just cute enough that I change my head shake into a nod.

"It's okay," I squeak. "Let's just move the quilt."

If I were anyone else, it would be a family heirloom. Since my family doesn't do quilts, I bought it at Goodwill. But it's precious to me.

"We can eat at the table," he says as he fires up my TV.

"Nope, this is…fun." My mother would be horrified. Maybe so would his ex. I like that idea and strip down to my panties and a tank top and climb onto the bed. "Let's do this."

"What was that evil little thought you just had?"

"Nothing."

He shoves his pants off and joins me, his gaze bright and knowing. "Not nothing." He cups my cheek, holding me in place as he searches my face. "Tell me."

"I was thinking…proper people don't do this."

"Ah. People like Madelyn?"

"And my mother."

"Good that you put them in the same category," he says. There's an edge to his voice, but it's not aimed at me.

"Yeah."

He tugs me into his lap. "You want to know anything about her?"

Yes. No. "I'm still struggling with the idea that you were engaged to her."

"You and me both. It was a mistake."

"I got the impression you aren't the marrying kind."

"I wasn't, and Maddie proved that point pretty hard core. Marrying her would have been a terrible mistake."

"Why?"

"I didn't love her."

"But you proposed to her."

"It wasn't...whatever fantasy you've concocted of a proposal. No grand gesture, no bended knee. It came up one day and it seemed like the obvious next step for us. My cousin is her best friend, we had common interests..."

"And when did it become obvious that it wasn't actually the next step for you?"

His jaw flexes and I wonder if I'm pushing too far. But he doesn't tense up or pull away. He gives me an embarrassed look. "She cheated on me."

"Oh." That's awful.

"She married the guy. He had me kicked out of the country. Super messy."

"Wow."

"We never would have gotten married. We couldn't pick a date...we never lived together...I mostly feel like an idiot because it took being cheated on to make me realize she wasn't the one for me."

"I'm sorry she hurt you."

"I'm not. Not anymore. It led me to you."

"Still..."

He shifts me to the side and opens the pizza box. "No still. Really, it was a learning experience, nothing more."

"What did you learn?"

He hands me a slice of pepperoni and mushroom and gives me a grin. "She's not someone I could eat pizza with naked."

I laugh, because we're not naked. Yet. But there's a kernel of truth there. I swallow hard. "Is that important to you?"

He licks a bit of pizza sauce off his thumb and grins as he leers at my boobs. "Feels pretty damn important, yeah."

"God, you're the dirtiest." But I'm grinning too, because warmth is filling my chest and spilling down my arms. This is happiness. And neither of us have had nearly enough of that in our lives.

We eat in companionable silence, watching something on the TV but I'm not following it at all, and neither is he. I keep turning over in my head what he said.

"What else is important to you?" I finally ask.

"This is enough. This is plenty."

"I know..." I take a deep breath. "But if I wanted to step outside my comfort zone and give you something else?"

His eyes light up. "Think I could keep my hands to myself if we went to a movie tomorrow night?"

"It would be a dark theatre. Why would you want to?"

"Is that a yes?"

"Depends what's playing." I reach for another piece of pizza and take a big-ass bite. "If nothing's good, maybe we could go to the mall. Get fries and sit in the food court."

He barks out a laugh. "So all the other kids in high school can see that we're going steady?"

"Isn't that what you want?"

He pinches the pizza out of my hand and pulls me on top of him, tugging the hand that he's gripping all the way to his mouth. He sucks off the pizza grease, then keeps sucking until my eyes go soft and my breath goes funny.

"Yes, I want to go steady with you, Ali."

Well, that's fucking terrifying. I swallow around the lump in my throat. "Okay."

"How close is my girlfriend to freaking out about the pizza sauce on her sheets?"

Less than I was before, because it makes my boyfriend happy, but I'm not going to give him that yet. That little bit of knowledge is just for me. I'd do anything to make him happy. Anything. And that's just a few steps away from losing myself completely, which is so not the plan. I shrug. "This is why we've got washing machines, right?"

He can't see the freakout in my head, thank God. He's just looking at me with the best look on his face, and I make myself focus on that. It's easier when he traces my bottom lip with his thumb.

Everything is easier when he's touching me. Grounding me.

I swipe at his thumb with my tongue, inviting him into my mouth. His eyelids droop as he slowly presses his thumb over my lips. "I like calling you that. My girlfriend. Like it gives me all sorts of special privileges."

I suck in response.

He growls.

I suck harder.

"Not that kind of special privilege, you minx."

I let go of his thumb with a wet pop that makes me slick between the legs. "You sure you don't want the boyfriend blow job?"

He groans. "How is it different?"

"I've been doing my Tumblr research."

"God yes."

I laugh as he falls back, his cock popping to attention.

Kissing my way down his chest, I lick his nipple, then the line of hair down the furrow between his ridged abs. It's narrow and sparse, then a little thicker right before I get to his erection. It smells like soap right now, but beneath it is a raw, masculine scent of skin and virility. Do all men smell this good? I'm guessing not.

And the fact that I don't know—and, Lord help me, I may never know—turns me on like nothing else.

I kiss my way down his shaft, pausing at the head to lick the pearly drop of pre-come there. I'm quite sure other men don't taste as good as him.

Sad to be other girls, then.

Awesome to be me.

"You taste yummy," I whisper, and he groans helplessly. I grin. The power of a blow job. And Tumblr promises me that if I trail kisses down the bottom of his cock, all the way to his balls...

My face heats up as I remember the rabbit hole I went down when I looked up why people shave their balls.

I keep going anyway. When I reach his sac, he rocks his hips. Oh good, he wants my lips there. But a dark thought crosses my mind. I don't want to ask him, of course. Jealousy has no place in the boyfriend blow job. It's a sex act of assuredness, one filled with the dirty deeds protected by the trust between two people who love each other.

But if that British skank sucked on Scott's balls...

Okay, being dirty maybe makes me petty.

Maybe.

Definitely.

I brush my lips over the tender skin in front of me and he shudders. Feigning an indifference I definitely don't feel, I ask, "Do you like having your balls sucked?"

He freezes. "Would you?"

"Answer the question."

"I've only imagined it, but yeah...fuck, yes."

"Nobody...?"

He groans and rocks his junk closer to my mouth.

Good enough for me.

In comparison to his thick erection, his nuts are smallish. I think. Maybe it's just by virtue of scale, like a walnut next to... Jesus, I don't even know what foodstuff to compare Scott's cock to. Zucchini sounds rude.

"Ali, suck on me." He's begging. Oh, I like that. Enough thinking. I soften my lips and open wide, sliding one ball into my mouth with my tongue.

He immediately makes his grunting, gonna-come noise, and his hand closes around his erection.

A tingly satisfaction ripples through me and I suck a little harder—just a little—to see if he likes that, too. He does. Thank you, Tumblr porn. Softly, I release him, and suck the other side into my mouth. Again, I work up to sucking hard, and again, he sounds close to coming.

And I haven't even worked on the relaxed-throat, how-deep-can-I-go game.

His hand is working pretty hard right now, but I want his come in my mouth. I want to suck him over the cliff and into oblivion. I shift a little higher, letting my boobs brush the insides of his thighs, then his wet balls. He shivers as my mouth finds the flared head of his cock, slick and coated with his pre-come.

About to be a hell of a lot slicker.

As his fist jerks down again, I swallow the top half of his cock. When he lets go, I replace his hand with mine.

His fingers tangle in my hair, and I let him set the pace. If he wants to fuck my face a little, he can. He's earned it. My circled fingers bump against my lips as I pump him up and down, catching a bit of spit each time until he's coated and it's all slick and smooth as he uses my mouth, faster and harder.

He growls my name. "Fuck, yeah, swallow my load. Oh, babe, your mouth..."

The first hot spurt takes me by surprise but I swallow the rest like a porn star, then clean him up with soft, gentle laps of my tongue. I kneel between his legs and grin at him, proud as a peacock. "Yeah?"

"Your turn," he growls, flipping me onto my back.

He spreads me open and dives right in, his tongue the first touch between my folds. No fingers, not foreplay to the fore-play. He's like a dying man at a pool of water, and who am I to deny him his fill?

I hitch my knees higher and prop myself up on my elbows.

It takes my breath away, this view of this giant man between my legs, his dark head bobbing as he sucks and licks and flicks me into bliss. "I want you to shave me again," I whisper as he teases the short curls there with his tongue.

"Anytime."

"Scott?"

He looks up. His face is wet. Oh God. This is so the wrong time.

"I love you." Three little words. The power to move moun-tains. I swear my world gets brighter, bigger as I say them, and then he's on top of me, sliding into me.

"I love you, Ali. Fuck, that's been a hard secret to keep."

"I'm sorry."

He groans as he thrusts into me. It really is better like this. There's a skin-on-skin drag that's raw and right. "Nothing to be sorry for. If it wasn't big and scary, it wouldn't be real."

"It is real, right?"

"Terrifyingly so." He kisses me, tracing the seam of my lips with the tip of his tongue. He tastes like me and I probably still taste like him. I shiver. "You're the one for me, Ali. This is as real as it gets, and I'm never letting you go."

I wrap my legs around him and rock my hips, bringing him deeper inside my belly. There's a bright, aching stretch inside as his cock nudges my cervix, as he finds space inside my body. "Sometimes you're gonna have to hold on tight."

"Like glue."

"I'm going to want to run away in a few months."

"Babe..." he kisses along my jaw and nips at my earlobe. "I can't wait to run away with you."

My heart might just explode. "What?"

He laces his fingers through mine and tugs my arms over my head, pinning me down. "I'm a bird on a wire, Ali. I'm ready to fly wherever you want to go."

Holding my gaze, he moves inside me, slow at first. Thick, drunk surges filled with love and promise. He ducks his head and finds my breasts, and I cry out as he pulls a nipple into his mouth. A tremor starts inside me, a slow, wobbling pleasure bubble that grows and flexes and shimmers in the heat he's stoking between us. I arch my back as he grazes my flesh with his teeth and his cock pushes ruthlessly through my slick folds.

"Come with me," I plea. I can feel myself squeezing him, begging him for his come inside me. He shifts his hands, pinning me down with one. The other finds my leg and presses me up and open, so he can slam into me harder. Faster. Deeper.

"Always." He growls my name, his face hard and intense as he watches me, watching him. He's on top of me, heavy and perfect, and this is all it takes, and I'm there.

"Yes," I cry out, and it's exactly right.

"Always," he repeats as he holds himself inside me, the aftershocks ripping between us.

Booty Call

Ali and Scott

part five

NEW YORK, AGAIN

[EPILOGUE 1]
ALISON

"To the birthday girl," Scott says, tipping his flute of prosecco against mine.

I give him a beaming smile. "Thank you."

After a six month international relations internship in Sydney, we're back in the States. I think we might head out to the west coast soon, because I'd like to do a masters degree in Asian Pacific politics, but that's a worry for another day. Another month.

This is our extended holiday. We had Christmas down under, and now we've been in New York for a month. We're subletting an apartment in SoHo and I'm doing some observerships at the United Nations, but New York is too close to both of our families for our comfort zone. Well, there's some debate over that.

My boyfriend likes to point out that I spend hours a week on the phone with both of my sisters. I point out that international telecommunications make that possible, and any time I want to see them, I can get on a jet plane.

But if we head out west, we'll be close to his brother Will. And Taylor, if she's still in Los Angeles by the time we settle. She's a bit of a bird on a wire, too.

I thought for sure she'd clash with Scott, because they're similar in a lot of ways, but when we stopped in L.A. on our way to Sydney, they totally hit it off. He needs to teach Hailey how to get along with Tay.

He was similarly afraid to introduce to me to Jeff. His brother is everything I hate about wealthy businessmen...but somehow he's different. I like the guy. I don't understand him, but I like him. It's all in how he looks at Scott, like he'd lay down his life for his older brother.

I know the feeling.

"I love you," I say, lacing my fingers into his. "Thank you for a magical birthday."

"It's not over yet," he says with a lazy, dirty grin.

"No?"

He winks. "I've got a surprise for you." He reaches into his pocket and pulls a pair of tickets and hands them over.

I squeal as I read the name of the show. "Broadway Burlesque?"

"Surprisingly not on Broadway."

I roll my eyes at him. "Ohmygod. This is amazing."

"We've got an hour before it starts. Want to walk?"

I tip my glass back and finish my wine. "Oh yeah."

We've done this every night that we've been in the city. Walked for blocks, hand-in-hand, and talked about...everything. Tonight we head down Prince Street. Scott tugs me to a stop in front of Agent Provocateur and whispers in my ear how turned on he was when I waved those panties in his face a year ago.

"Oh yeah?"

"I wanted to take you over my knee and spank you, though."

"Maybe we should do that tonight." I lick my lips. "Turn my bottom pink. A belated punishment for teasing you."

"Punishment?" He crushes his mouth against mine and I tug on his hips. I want the full weight of him against me. I always want it all, no holding back. "Babe, I should thank you every single day for being so persistent."

"Then you're welcome. Will you please spank me?"

He laughs and squeezes my ass. "One hundred percent."

"Where do you want to walk tonight?" I ask him as we step off again.

"There's a garden up ahead I found last week," he says. "Full of statues. It's kind of cool."

I grin up at him. "Awesome."

We turn right at Elizabeth Street. It's dark and quiet, although there's traffic just a block away. The street lights glow, though, and up ahead I see a fence. "Is that it?"

"Yeah," he says. "This is it."

As we reach it, I realize the glow is coming from inside the garden, too. Hundreds of lanterns are hung from tree branches and perched beside the statues.

"Wow," I breathe.

Scott wraps his arms around me from behind. "Happy birthday," he whispers. "I'm sorry I fucked up the last one."

I shake my head. "All a part of our journey, babe."

He squeezes me tight, then takes my hand and leads me deeper into the garden. It's positively magical.

"I think this might be the best birthday I've ever had," I whisper, turning in a slow circle. A fat, lazy snowflake drifts in front of me, and I look up at the sky. "It's going to snow tonight, huh?"

"We can stay in bed all day tomorrow," Scott says from behind me. "Celebrating, I hope."

I turn around.

He's down on one knee, holding a ring in his hand.

I don't cry. Not unless my heart is broken.

And apparently, when I'm proposed to. "What are you doing?"

He grins at me. "Taking a really big risk, because I don't want to fuck up another birthday."

I laugh weakly, swiping at my wet cheeks. "Okay."

"Ali, the last year has been the best of my life. You are the best in my life. The best late nights and early mornings. The best texts, the best jokes, the best serious conversations." He looks up at the sky. "The best walks. The best adventures. I want to share all of that with you, for the rest of my life."

"Okay."

He reaches for me with his other hand and I stumble forward, squeezing my fingers around his. "Will you be wife? The mother of my children and the savior of my world?"

"That's a big ask," I mumble through the tears.

"The kids can wait a while if you want."

I shake my head. "That's not the big ask. Of course I want to have your babies, you dork. Yes, I'll marry you. Yes, I'll share my adventures with you. Yes, yes, yes. I need you by my side, always and forever."

He slides the ring onto my finger before tugging me onto his lap. "Forever sounds perfect."

MAY, TWO YEARS LATER

His palm drifts under my t-shirt, light strokes on my belly the signal he wants me to wake up. I will, but I'm

———

———

Taylor's story is coming soon! Wicked Sin will release March 26, 2019. And you can loop back to start at the beginning if you haven't read Cole and Hailey's story, Hate F*@k. (Seriously get on that, because you need Cole's dirty mouth in your life!)

The Forbidden Bodyguards Series

Hate F*@k (Cole and Hailey)
Booty Call (Ali and Scott)
Dirty Love (Wilson and Tabitha)

Wicked Sin (Taylor and Luke)
Filthy Liar (Jason and Melinda)

www.ainsleybooth.com

the **Frisky Beavers** series

co-written with Sadie Haller

Prime Minister

Dr. Bad Boy

Full Mountie

Mr. Hat Trick

Page of Swords

Bull of the Woods

the **Pine Harbour** series

writing as Zoe York

Love in a Small Town

Love in a Snow Storm

Love on a Spring Morning

Love on a Summer Night

Love on the Run

Love in a Sandstorm

Love on the Outskirts of Town

ACKNOWLEDGMENTS

Sadie Haller has been my first reader since the very first Hate F*@k serial part. I love that she loves my dirty heroes and my lippy heroines as much as I do, and I'm grateful beyond words that she drops everything to fact check and comma check and do the occasional real life choreography check, too. I don't believe any Mr. Hallers were injured in the making of this book, thank goodness.

Maria Rose gets my second sincere thanks for her amazingly quick turnaround on proofreading. A reader who can catch a missing article in the middle of a sex scene is a valuable friend indeed.

My Ainsley's Angels Facebook group. I'm sorry I'm so quiet most of the time. I promise it's because I'm busy creating filthy scenes for your favorite characters.

Every single reader who loved Hate F*@k and has been waiting a year for more from this world. I promise the next one won't take me another year.

My husband, for being proud of everything I write. Even the fisting scene. Sorry if anyone asks you about it. You can tell them I saw it on Tumblr. Your call if you want to share my secret inspiration board. I love you. Stop blushing.

~ Ainsley

www.ainsleybooth.com

ABOUT THE AUTHOR

Ainsley Booth is a USA Today bestselling author of more than fifty romances between this pen name and her alter-ego, Zoe York. She lives in London, Ontario, Canada with her family.

facebook.com/ainsleyboothwrites

instagram.com/ainsleyboothwrites

9 781926 527710